THE MAKING OF A LEGEND:

NEEK'S RISE TO FAME

BY

DIANA CARTER

THE MAKING OF A LEGEND:

NEEK'S RISE TO FAME

D I A N A   C A R T E R

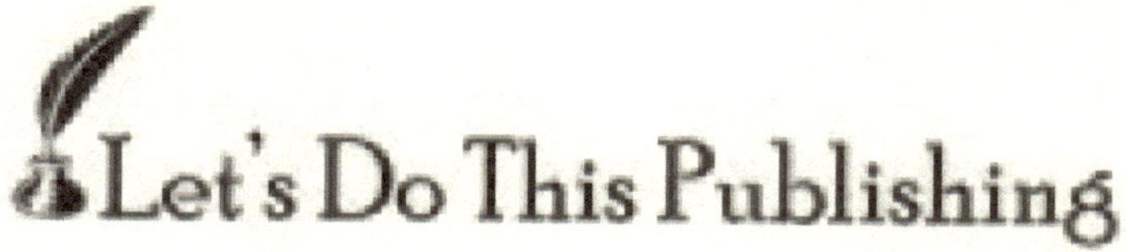

P.O. Box 300795
Drayton Plaines, MI 48330
ldtpllc@gmail.com

The Making of a Legend: Neek's Rise to Fame

Family Drama/Relationships

LET'S DO THIS PUBLISHING, LLC
P.O. Box 300795
Drayton Plaines, MI 48330

ISBN 13: 9781733154840

OTHER BOOKS WRITTEN BY DIANA CARTER

BROKEN PROMISES SERIES

Broken Promises: Shattered Dreams
When Shattered Dreams Become Reality
Shattered Dreams The Final Chapter
In The Name of Justice: The Erica Blackstone Chronicles

DARK REVENGE SERIES

The Trey Taylor Story
When Time Runs Out: Tara's Quest for Vengeance
TJ The Forgotten Brother

The Sister Factor Series

Diamond's Fight for Justice
Dior's Darlings Daycare
Kristina's Kozy Korner
Krystal's House of Secrets
Never a Dull Moment: The Nick Jr. Story

Single Titles

The Candidate: The Race to the Top
Unbreakable: When Two Hearts Become One

Dedication

This book is dedicated to a special lady that promised to read my next book if I wrote about basketball, Annie McGee. Annie inspired me to write yet again about something outside of my comfort zone. This was by far the hardest book I've written in my writing career. I thank Annie for giving me the main characters of this book along with part of the plot line. I now know more about basketball then I wanted to know, but this book was a good learning experience. Geared towards the younger audience, I hope this book brings inspiration to those who think because you may have grown up in less than acceptable surroundings don't mean that is where you will end up. I would also like to give a shout out to my two youngest sons Kamal and Jimmy Jr. that help me immensely with the ins and out of the basketball world. With their help I was able to make the main character the great person he became.

Acknowledgements

God has been a major part of my life. He has been the one who has never let me down. I find strength in knowing that all will be well if I continue to put him first in my life. As I continue to write books in the future, I hope they would bring comfort and entertainment to readers young and old. To round out the year, I'm working on a sequel to **Unbreakable** (my first romance novel). I am also working on another book that is expected to be published this year about human trafficking. This is a real problem today that impacts young girls that are vulnerable to older men.

To change things up a little, I like to say how proud I am of myself. People generally don't take the time out to praise what they have brought into others' lives. As I continue to grow and change, I see that sticking to my beliefs and goals have paid off. I may not be where I want or need to be financially, but I can say that I'm proud of the mother, grandmother, sister, aunt, and friend I have become to people that are important in my life. There were challenges I've had to deal with at times that were overwhelming, but my faith and focus kept me going on the right path.

My advice is never to be afraid to give yourself credit for accomplishments you've made in life, or the ones you continue to make. Always keep in mind that God's will is all you need to reach any goal you set in life. In closing I would like to give praise to my oldest son, DeAndre. He has been such a blessing to many people, especially young people through his motivational speaking and the giving of himself. His best and greatest accomplishment is the great dad he is to his daughter, Savannah Grace. She is well on her way to be as successful as her dad.

God's blessing,

Diana Carter

Chapter One

Neek sat in his small bedroom wondering what he should do with the rest of his life. The twenty-one-year-old University of Mercy senior had some major decisions to make. Several pro teams have been chasing the highly sought-after point guard for years. The promise he made to his dad before he passed away four years ago weighed heavily on his mind. He promised his dad he wouldn't leave school until he gotten his bachelor's degree. The engineering major was torn because if he decided to go pro now he would be able to support his hard-working mom, Willimena (Willa for short) and two younger siblings Desiree (aka Desi) and Xavier (aka X). Not to mention it would please his demanding girlfriend, Monica Jackson. He'd been home for summer break for a few days.

His decision wouldn't be so as hard if he didn't feel responsible for his mom and siblings. Growing up in the hood was a tough life. Desi was five years younger than Neek while X was eleven years younger. They had a hard time of it since their mom became involved with X's dad who was now serving a life sentence in prison for murdering his oldest child mama. Willa lost her way when she couldn't persuade Neek and Desi's dad, James Domineek Williamson (JD), to come back home. He refused to come back home or grant her the divorce she wanted. When Willa realized she wasn't going to be able to convince her husband to come home, she started hanging out with Xavier Grant Porter (Peanut) a local thug.

For nearly four years Willa's relationship with Peanut took over her life. She went from a loving and caring mom and wife to a homeless crack head with no direction or goals in her life. Off and on over the next four years, Willa had setbacks but now for the last two years she has been clean. It was right on time because when she lost her mom, Willow to cancer six months ago it was tragic. During the times when Willa was on the streets it was Willow that came to the rescue of her three grandchildren. She was their rock. When she passed away Neek was down for quite some time. Willa's dad passed away when she was a young child and Willow never remarried.

Willow's death sent Desi into a tail spin. All the siblings were more attached to their grandmother than their mom. Desi was always the sibling most likely to be lost to the rough street life in their challenging Detroit neighborhood. Desi was headstrong and feisty. Since their grandmother passed away she didn't listen to or respect anyone, but Neek. Even Neek had a rough go of it to keep his sister on the straight and narrow. She was one of those impulsive girls that acted before she thought the entire situation through. Neek had to come to her rescue more than once when she found herself in over her head.

On the other hand, X put more pressure on Neek than anyone else in the family without even knowing what he was doing. X had this hero worshipper thing going on. He thought the world started and ended with Neek. He was upset when Neek became busy with his college life and time spent with Monica. X looked at Neek as a father figure since his dad wasn't in the picture and JD didn't accept him. Neek wanted to be a role model to his little brother but with less time and the prospect of signing with the NBA made his choice more difficult.

If Neek was honest with himself, he would have to admit, Monica was the biggest reason why he wanted to sign with the NBA. Holding on to Monica had become just as important as his family, school, and career. Monica wanted to get out of the hood sooner rather than later. She was getting restless and wanted the good life of fame and fortune the NBA would provide.

Also, another concern was his best friend, Donnell Wright (Nell). Neek feared Nell would fall prey to their former friend Jefferson Peterson (Ghost) a well-known and feared drug dealer. Nell mostly stayed away from Ghost since he was attending University of Michigan (U of M) and only returned home for holidays and the summer. When he was home Ghost made it his goal to pull Nell into his world. Nell and Ghost were friends before they met Neek, so Ghost felt dissed when Nell stop hanging out with him. Neek was able to encourage Nell to stay on the right side of the law, but it was a tough battle because like Monica, Nell was ready to run from the hood.

Neek was tired of sitting around pondering over his problems. He decided to once again seek the advice of this mentor and his dad's best friend Pastor Nathanial Magee. Pastor Nate had a way of convincing you to make the right decisions without forcing his opinions onto you. After Neek showered and dressed, he ran out the door leaving his demons behind him to talk to Pastor Nate before he lost his mind.

Pastor Nathanial Magee, Senior Pastor at First Baptist Church sat at his desk in his office waiting on a young man that had the abilities to change so many lives for the best. A lot of weight was placed on this young man's shoulders. Losing his dad in his most vulnerable years was a big set-back. Pastor Nate thought about his best friend that lost his life so long ago, leaving behind two biological children and one step child that he never paid attention to because of his relationship with his estranged wife. The damage JD's passing had on his children was still a factor in their lives they were finding hard to overcome.

Pastor Nate was shocked that JD didn't make provisions for his family upon his death. JD was a long-distance truck driver that made good money, but in the end, there was barely enough money to give him a proper burial. There was life insurance that basically paid off the house while all the time Willa thought JD was working for a company he was basically picking up odd jobs here and there. This made the already stressed Willa to further spin out of control. Which put more pressure on Neek to take care of his family while attending University and pondering whether to sign with the NBA.

For the first time in his pastoral career he was at odds where there was no simple solution to one of his parishioner's problems. Neek was like a son to him, so Pastor Nate wanted to tread carefully before advising this young man on a decision that will follow him for the rest of his life. In previous sessions with Neek, Pastor Nate tried to caution him on basing his life changing decisions on others including his mom. The knock at his door alerted Pastor Nate that Neek had arrived.

"Hi, Pastor Nate thanks for seeing me on short notice." Neek said as he sat down in one of the chairs that were in front of Pastor Nate's desk.

"My door is always open to you and your family, Domineek." Pastor Nate said.

"We really appreciate all that you have done for us over the years since my dad passed away."

"My pleasure, Son, your dad was one of my dearest friend. Sometimes I think his smiling face will walk through that door at any minute."

"It's, Mom and Desi that I feel bad for. I know my parents probably never would have gotten back together, but I held out hope that they would. Desi in still spiraling out of control since dad and grandma died."

"Domineek, we all have demons that follow us no matter how hard we try to shake them loose. JD's demons were something that he didn't understand so instead of sticking around and working on them, he chose to try to run away from them.,"

"Pastor, I know my mom isn't a saint, but I just couldn't understand why dad wouldn't just let her go since he didn't want to be with her any longer, it wasn't fair to keep her hanging."

"Deep down, son your dad wanted your mom back, but he couldn't give her what she needed. It tore him apart when she took up with that Peanut character. Since I have limited time today can we get to the real reason you're here, Son?"

A sad look appeared across Neek's face. "Pastor Nate, I don't know what to do. I'm feel like I'm being pulled is so many directions at once that it's driving me crazy."

"Does this have to do with your decision to sign with the NBA?"

"You're right in one guess. At first the only goal I was focused on was finishing my degree, so I could honor my dad's wishes, but the struggles me and my family are going through tells me that I need to make money, so I can provide them with a better life."

"Where do you come into this picture, Domineek?"

"I don't understand your question, Pastor Nate."

"From today and our previous conversations you mentioned that you wanted to help your mom, siblings, girlfriend, best friend, and keep your promise to your dad. Where do you fit in all of this?"

"It hurts me I'm away from home so much and mom has to work two jobs to support the family. I want to be there for them more, but with school and my basketball schedule it's not possible."

"Answer this for me, Domineek. What would your life be like if you didn't try to look out for all the people you care about?"

"That's easy. My one passion since I was four years old was to be the best point guard in the NBA history." Neek said with a big smile on his face.

"What would happen if you didn't make that promise to your dad and the people you love weighing on you?"

"That's easy too. I would weigh my options and be a Detroit Pistons. I know I can get more money and a better deal with other teams, but I'm a hometown boy at heart and I would like to help make my home team better."

Studying the young man sitting in front of him, Pastor Nate thought carefully before speaking. "Do you feel you just answered your own question of what decision you should make?"

"Most of the time I make the decision, but then I see dad's face staring at me in disappointment. That's not my only issue, engineering is also a passion of mine. I wish there was an option to do both."

"Domineek, I'm sure if you made the decision to go pro any team would be agreeable to assisting you in completing your education. Remember your worth, son."

"I do, Pastor Nate. I just don't want to get so caught up in all the hype that finishing school becomes a nonissue."

"I tell you what. Think about what we've talked about over the last few months and see me after church on Sunday."

"Thanks, Pastor Nate. I feel so much better already. I know I can't fix everyone's problems in my life, but if I can do right by my family I would feel so much better. I don't want to leave them behind."

"See you on Sunday, son. Remember the end goal is to do what is best for you to do right by others."

"I got you, Pastor Nate. Enjoy the rest of your week." Neek gave the pastor some dap before leaving his office.

Chapter Two

Neek had a few days to think over his meeting with Pastor Nate. He now wanted to talk to his mom about the situation. He was glad they would have some alone time for about an hour before she had to go to work. X was at a stay over at his friend's house and Desi had already left for her summer job. He was going to meet up with Monica for lunch. She was getting restless and couldn't understand why Neek was having such a tough time make his decision. The contract and signing bonus he would get if he joined the NBA would give the family more money than they ever dreamed of. Hearing his mom about to enter the kitchen Neek took a deep breath.

"Good morning, Mama."

"Morning, babe, why are you up so early?"

"I need to talk to you in private about a decision I've made."

"Let me take a seat, babe. This sounds serious." Willa took a seat across from Neek.

"Mama, I met with Pastor Nate a few days ago. We've been talking a lot lately. Thinking about our situation and many other factors I've decided to join the NBA."

Neek was sadden when there was a shock look on Willa's face. "Babe, I thought you wanted to finish school first. I see the writing on the wall. This is all about that girl." Willa said.

"No, Mama. Don't blame my decision on Monica."

"Babe, you only have one more year to go. You avoided making this decision for this long. Those people have been hounded you since you left high school. Why give in now?"

"Mama, my biggest reason is because I want to do right by you, Desi, and X. If we stay in this neighborhood we're going to lose Desi."

"Desi will be alright. You shouldn't worry about her issues. You have a lot on your plate. This summer should be about getting ready for your last year of college."

"Mama, I'm going to find a way to do both. I haven't forgotten my promise to dad."

"It's good you want to honor your dad, but you love engineering. You have been passionate about this since you were a kid."

"I'm in a good position to do both, Mama. Over the next few weeks I will be working with Nell, Pastor Nate, and Coach Rodgers to find the best agent that will ensure I can finish my degree on time. We have set up a meeting with a top-grade sports agent."

"So, this is a done deal. You're leaving school." Willa asked sadly.

"Yes, Mama, please be happy for me. I want to give all of us the kind of life we deserve."

"Thanks for giving me a heads up, babe. I have to get to work now."

"Before you go, Mama, think about what you want to do with your life now that you won't have to work much longer. Let's look at the positive things my decision would bring into all our lives."

"Okay, babe, see you later."

Neek stood and pulled his mom gently out of her chair. He whispered softly into her ear. "Mama, I love you. We deserve better." Slightly kissing her on her forehead, Neek eyes followed his mom as she left out of the back door.

As Neek waited on Monica to join him for lunch, he thought about how strangely she was acting since he'd been home. He knew she was upset with him because he couldn't decide on whether he would join the NBA. She was the one that wanted to have lunch today. He hoped he would find out what was on her mind. Thinking back to his conversation with his mom earlier today, he was sad that she and Monica didn't get along. His mom didn't see any redeeming qualities in Monica. Monica didn't like his mom either, saying she was using him to be a dad to his clinging siblings.

Seeing Monica walk through the restaurant door brought a big smile to Neek's face. He loved her more and more each day. He felt so blessed the day he met her. She was like a breath of fresh air on a breezy sunny day. He stood when she reached the table, so he could pull her chair out. The bright yellow jumper she wore made her cinnamon skin glow. Her natural light brown eyes and curly hair was on point. As the waitress approached the table he stared at Monica fixated on her beauty.

"Do you know what you want to order, sweetie?" Neek asked in a soft sexy voice.

"I'm not that hungry. Soup and salad would do for me." Monica replied.

"Sweetie, if you weren't hungry we could have met at my house. No one is home right now."

"Neek, I needed to see you in a different environment."

"What do you mean by a different environment?" Neek asked puzzled.

"I need for you to listen closely to me, Neek."

"Okay, I'm listening."

"Neek, you know I love you, but lately our lives seem to be moving in different directions."

"I'm not understanding you, sweetie." Neek wanted to hurry to tell Monica their struggles would be over soon.

"We were young when we met, Neek. I'm thinking at the time the relationship worked because we filled a void in each other lives, but now that we have grown that growth has moved us in different directions."

"This is nonsense, Monica. We've had our challenges, but we've gotten through them just fine."

"That's where we differ. I've been struggling to figure out what I want out of life. I haven't gotten everything worked out yet, but I know what I want and need. I need to do this on my own."

"Why are you talking like I've been holding you back from your dreams. I've been your biggest supporter, Monica."

"Neek, you're not hearing me. I need to be on my own."

"But things are about to get better for us. I…"

Monica held up her hand to stop Neek from talking. "I'm sorry, Neek. Our relationship is over. I need to move on in a different direction in my life.

Neek couldn't believe what he was hearing. After wrestling with the biggest decision in his life and coming up with a solution that would help everyone he loves, the person he thought he would spend the rest of his life with wanted out. Before he could find the words to make Monica change her mind, with tears in her eyes she stood and ran out the door she came in only a few minutes earlier.

Chapter Three

The last few days had been the worse in Neek's life. He still couldn't get over the fact that Monica left him. Just when he thought things would go his way, she had to drop that bombshell on him. It was hard for him to speak about this to anyone. The only person he told was Nell. He wanted to talk to his mom about it but was afraid she would do a happy dance because she never thought Monica was right for him. The same could be said for his sister, Desi she didn't like Monica neither, but she was able to tolerate her more than his mom. Now that one of the main factors for his turning pro was out the door, Neek wondered if he was making the right decision. He didn't know if God was trying to send him a message that he wasn't making the right decision.

Neek's mood didn't change when he heard rumors that Monica left him for Ghost. He knew his family and others would find out he was dumped, but he wished he had time to heal and adjust to this new situation. His mom and sister knew he was dealing with something major but decided not to press the issue until he was ready to talk to them. X was a different story. His innocence didn't stop him from asking tons of questions as to why his hero was so sad. He knew he had to pull himself together soon. When he get into moods like this, he would calm himself down by thinking about his early childhood.

The Early Years

Neek wondered why his parents argued so much. His dad made a lot of money, but that wasn't enough. They still stayed in a bad part of Detroit. He remembers his mom fussing saying she wanted to move out of the ghetto, but his dad saying they were fine where they were at. He further explained that investing in their children was more important than living beyond their means. Neek didn't care about any of that he was just happy that by the time he was six years old he got the chance to go to his first basketball camp. His dad worked with him since he was four years old on his ball handling and concentration.

His dad always talked to him about beef. At a young age Neek didn't know what that meant but knew it must be important because his dad told him never to forget the beef. Once beef was drilled into his head his dad went on to C for concentration and awareness. By the time Neek was eight years old and had been to all sorts of basketball training camps he finally understood that what beef and C meant in the basketball world. Beef meant balance, eyes, elbow, and follow through. Balance was important before you shoot. Eyes were keeping your eyes on the ball while you shoot. Elbow was to make sure you keep them close to our body when you shoot. Follow through on your shot, your hand should look like you're reaching inside a cookie jar.

Sometimes Neek used to get mad at his dad because he had to practice basketball every day and never got the chance to play with his friends. Neek loved basketball but he also like working with numbers. That when he found his second love, engineering. His tough basketball schedule didn't bother him until he was ten and he met his best friend, Donnell (Nell). Nell was okay at basketball, but it wasn't his main focus like it was with Neek. A year later when Nell's then best friend moved into the neighborhood, Jefferson Peters (Ghost), the three boys became best of friends. They did everything together until they got a little older and Ghost wanted to do wild things the other two boys wasn't cool with.

When that started happening Neek's dad refused to let Neek hang around with the other boys. It took Neek more than six months to convince his dad that Nell wasn't like Ghost. Ghost started making trouble for the other two boys because they refused to hang out with him because of his unlawful actions. He tried to bribe them with money and material things and when that didn't work he started rumors with the other neighborhood kids to turn them against Neek and Nell. The boys didn't care because at this stage, Neek and Donnell had already made plans for high school and college. Neek was getting lots of attention with his basketball skills while Nell was just as successful with his computer skills.

Remembering his dad's support was something Neek was always able to count on. Before he entered high school, he had been to several basketball camps. Sometimes Neek use to get upset with his mom because she always fussed about his dad spending too much money on Neek's basketball activities and Desi's dance classes. The fights had gotten worse as they grew older and their expenses cost more. When their dad finally moved out that's when Willa lost her way.

His dad wasn't in the city as much after his parents separated, but when he was he made sure to practice with Neek. Even when he wasn't around he drilled into Neek that practicing was the only way to hone his skills. When he wasn't around he wanted Neek to focus on his concentration and being aware of what was going on around him. He told Neek this was the most important part of shooting. With awareness his dad explained to him, he would know about other players' position on the court and options and plays without consciously hearing their steps. Another big part of concentration was not having too much of what they call 'rear-view mirror' thinking about what is behind you or in your blind spots. The hardest part for Neek was learning that using peripheral vision should be automatic.

The greatest accomplishment Neek could remember from all the training in his younger years was learning how to shoot with one hand. It took him years to perfect this skill. He practiced this skill more than the concentration that his dad said was so important. A close second behind shooting with one hand was learning how to shoot with his non-dominant hand. Since Neek was left handed and his dad was right sometimes it was hard to learn how to shoot from his dad's angle. It was easier in the camps he went to because basically they would pair the children up with whichever coach had the dominant hand.

Neek was thinking about the Kill Drill his dad, basketball camps, and high school/college coaches force upon him. This is a full-court, down and back timed drill that prepares a player to build his/her stamina. With ninety-seconds on the clock this is a feat that is be difficult for any player that is out of shape. Coming out of his blast into the past, Neek was irritated when someone knocked at his bedroom door. He wanted to yell go away but instead he asked who was on the other side of the door. When Pastor Nate announced himself Domineek was shaken.

Getting up to open his door, Neek said, "Pastor Nate, I wasn't expecting you."

"That's ok, Neek. I was in the neighborhood and decided to stop by. Is this a bad time for you?"

"No, sir, I was just thinking about my earlier days of basketball. I guess my mom told you about my decision to turn pro."

"No, she didn't. I wanted to see how you were holding up. I can't betray and confidences, but I heard about your situation with Monica."

"There is no situation. She flat out dumped me." Neek said in an angry tone.

"I know this is very hurtful to you, Neek."

"Yes, it is. The sad part about it was I didn't get the chance to tell her I was turning pro. I knew that would have made a difference in her decision to leave me."

"That's hard to say, Neek. You told me on more than one occasion that Monica was restless. Maybe she was just ready to get out of the relationship."

"Yeah out with me and in with that Ghost fool."

"You don't know that to be true. Or did she tell you this?"

"No, she didn't have the guts to be honest with me. I know she must have been seeing him behind my back because there is no way she would start up with him days after she walked out on me."

"Neek, I know all of this is hard on you, but you must focus on all the progress you have made in your young life."

"Pastor Nate, I'm scared I'll never be able to get pass this hurt and anger. All I can think about or see when I close my eyes is hearing her voice and seeing her walking out on me saying we grew apart."

"Maybe you should just take this at face value. Your life moved on after you guys graduated from high school. Monica completed one year at Wayne State and decided she wasn't cut out for university life. Slowly she has changed but since your schedule has been so full you haven't notice she was slipping away."

"Hold up a minute, Pastor Nate. Have you been talking to Monica?"

"You know I can't tell you that. Just like you, I hear the rumors going around. I just don't want you to lose your way after this difficult blow."

"Thanks for stopping by, Pastor Nate. I really appreciate your concern. I'm not going to do anything stupid."

"That's good to hear, son. I'm just a phone call away if there is anything I can do for you. Stay strong and walk in God's footsteps."

"Can you pray for me before you leave, Pastor Nate?"

"Certainty I can, Domineek."

After the prayer, Neek walked the Pastor to the door and said, "You don't know how much it means to me that you have faith in me Pastor Nate." Neek said as he waved bye to the Pastor from his front door.

Chapter Four

Neek sat in Coach Rodger's office. As he sat there knowing it may be his last time sadden him. The three years he spent under Coach Rodgers's leadership made him the skillful basketball player he was today. He owed the coach so much, especially listening to him complaining about the possibility of losing Monica. He wondered since the word was out if the coach had already heard about the breakup. He felt off asking the coach for help with turning pro. Coach Rodgers was of the same mind as his dad, get your education first. He thought making the decision to leave school would give him peace of mind, but it didn't. He thought it was because he was still upset about Monica.

The weekend didn't go well. Finally having a sit down with his mom Saturday night was exhausting. Even though she didn't express it, Neek knew she was happy that he and Monica had split. He was frustrated because his mom didn't have foot to stand on when it came to relationships after she got involved with Peanut. Even before he went to prison for life, he didn't take care of X. At first his mom used to try to force the issue until she realized she was wasting her time. Fortunate enough to have another alone time with his mom, Neek poured out his heart to her.

"Mama, I'm sorry for being down over the last few days."

"What's wrong, Neek?" Willa asked already knowing the answer.

"If you haven't already heard, Monica dumped me."

"Really, when and why did she do that?"

"It happened a few days ago. She said that we have grown apart.*"*

"Babe, I'm going to be honest with you. I'm so sorry for the pain you must be going through, but in the end, this is the best thing that could have happened to you."

"Mama, I don't want to hear that right now."

"I know you don't, but you need to hear it."

"I didn't even get the chance to tell her that I decided to go pro."

Willa laughed so hard Neek thought she had lost her mind. "Mama this isn't funny."

"Yes, the hell it is. I bet that heifer is going to regret her decision big time once she hears your news."

"No matter what you think about her, Mom, Monica loved me."

"If she loved you so much why did she dump you?"

"She has grown without me, Mama."

"No, I can tell you what she is all about and that's living the high life. She been bugging the shit out of you to go pro ever since you have been scouted by the recruiters.

"Mama, she isn't the only one that wants a better lifestyle. I've been wanting to get us out of this neighborhood since I graduated from high school."

"But the difference between the two of you is that you have dedicated yourself to finishing your education which will be something you can rely on in the future."

"Mama, you said yourself that school isn't for everyone. Okay, Monica didn't finish school, but at least she tried."

"Why are you still taking up for her when she broke your heart?"

"Love don't just disappear, Mama, you should know that better than anyone. I know that you still loved dad even after he left us."

"This isn't about me, boy. It's about how lucky you are that heifer walked out on you. She should have stood by your side until things gotten better."

"Well, that's not here or there right now, Mama."

That was the farthest Neek gotten into his conversation with his mom before Coach Rodgers walked into the office. He was a man that always had a smile on his face no matter the situation. He was always encouraging his students to do better for themselves. Neek wished he had met the coach before his dad died. They probably would have been friends because they had a similar teaching style when working out with him. Neek greeted the coach.

"Good morning, Coach Rodgers. How is your day going?"

"It's going well. What brings you by today? I thought I wouldn't see you until you came back to school. I know you had big plans for you and Monica over the summer."

Sadness spread across Neek's face. "I guess you haven't heard. Monica dumped me."

"Man, I'm sorry to hear that. Do you want to talk about it?"

"There's not much to talk about. My mom is thrilled about it. My brother wonders why I'm down, and my sister is so wrapped up in her lifestyle, I don't think she notices anything that is going on around her."

"Neek did this really come as a surprise to you. You told me more than once that Monica was acting differently towards you."

"I know, but I thought she was just tired of living the humble life. I was just about to tell her some great news."

"Neek don't do this. You only have one more year to go."

"I'm sorry, Coach. If I don't get my family out of the hood we're going to lose my sister to the streets. My brother isn't going to fare any better."

"What about the promise you made to your dad?"

"I will keep my promise. I love engineering as much as I do basketball, but me and my family need financial security right now."

"How do you plan to finish school once you go pro? The NBA isn't going to care about seeing that you finish your education."

"That's why I'm here. I need you to help me to ensure I don't get taken advantage of when signing my contract."

"Neek, I'm not a sports agent or attorney. You will need both to protect your interest."

"I was thinking that if I get the right team together we can make sure I get an agent that will look out for me. I want you, me, Pastor Nate, and Nell to be a part of that team."

"Neek don't give into the pressure these teams are placing on you. Believe me they will want you just as badly next year."

"I know it was important to my dad for me to finish my degree, but it was just as important that I get into the NBA. He sacrificed a lot for me and Desi. All of that could come to fruition it I can financially provide for my family."

"How much does this decision have to do with your breakup with Monica?"

"It has nothing at all to do with Monica. She broke it off with me before I could tell her my decision."

"Have you prayed on this, Neek?"

"Yes, I have. I also had Pastor Nate to pray with me. He isn't sure I'm making the right decision, but he want me to think about it long and hard to make sure I'm doing it for me and not just to satisfy a need to my family."

"I'll tell you what. I will investigate this for you. Hang tight for right now. I will contact you within a few days."

"Thanks, Coach Rodgers. I really appreciate your help."

"While you're waiting on me to get back to you weigh the pros and cons of this decision. Remember you're not just a great basketball player, but you're also a great student, son, brother, and friend. Stay strong brother."

"I will never forget the confidence you have instilled in me, Coach Rodgers. I'll talk to you in a few days." Neek stood and gave his coach for the last three years a firm handshake before leaving his office.

Chapter Five

Neek was having another bad day. He spent most of yesterday with Nell. On top of his own problems, Nell was approached by Ghost again to come work for him. Financially Nell's family was worse off than Neek's. The money and power offered by Ghost was tempting for the out of work computer geek. Since Nell been home he has been looking for a job but hasn't been successful so far. Remembering their conversation, Neek drove home to his troubled friend that they all will be okay once he turned pro.

"Nell, man you got to stay away from that crazy dude."

"I know, Neek. Sometimes I lose myself and what I don't have instead of appreciating that I have three years of college under my belt."

"That's what I'm talking about. I need you to be on my team. Basketball is a cut throat industry. I need people around me I can trust. Coach Rodgers is looking into sports agents. Pastor Nate will round off my power group."

"Wow, Nell. I don't know how you do it. I know your heart is still crushed from what Monica did to you."

"It still hurts like hell, but I know God has a lot in store for me. I just hope I'm strong enough to chase her away when she comes running back to me when I start making money."

"And you know as sure as the nose on your face she will come running. That is if Ghost lets her."

"So, I guess the rumors are true. Monica is hanging out with Ghost."

"Yeah, man, the only thing I will give her credit for is that she broke things off with you before she moved in with him."

Neek was shocked. "Monica is shacking with that fool?"

"I'm sorry, Neek. I thought you knew."

"So, I guess the rumors are also true that she has been seeing Ghost for over a year?"

"I'm not sure how long, Neek."

"When did you find out, Nell?"

"Find out what?"

"That Monica was stepping out on me."

"Only recently I've heard some rumors. I don't believe every rumor I hear. I know you guys loved each other so I didn't take any of what I heard at face value."

"All I know is I hope she knows what she is getting herself into. Fast money is the worse money you can come across."

"Man, I think she is going to have to find that out the hard way."

"I'm going to turn in, Nell. I'll holla at you about the sports agent as soon as I hear from Coach Rodgers." Neek walked Nell to the door and headed back upstairs so he could rest his eyes.

Neek came back to the present. It was good to talk to Nell yesterday. He hoped he would do as he was promised and stay away from Ghost. Ghost was bad news. Neek couldn't believe they shared so much together when they were younger and now they couldn't stand being in the same room with each other. Neek knew that Ghost must feel vindicated since he had Monica. He had tried on many different occasions to take her away from Neek. Now that he has succeeded, Neek knew he wouldn't wait too long to rub his face into it. Neek was shaken out of his daydreams when there was a knock on his bedroom door.

"Come in." Neek shouted.

"Hey, big brother, how are you?" Desi said as she flopped down in the chair that was at Neek's desk."

"What's up, Desi?"

"I wanted to see how you were doing. I never get to see you except on Fridays when I don't have to work."

"I'm good, just chilling."

"I know that's not true. You know I can go and beat the hog shit out of that tramp if you want me to."

"No that's not what I want, Desi. What I want is to know how are doing and if you talked to Mama?"

"You know she doesn't talk to me she talks at me, but she hasn't done that in a while. Is something going on?"

"Yes, but I need you to keep this on the down low until I can get things ironed out."

"Do tell. I need to get my mind off that retarded job."

"Mama isn't happy about it, but I decided to go pro."

"No, Neek. Please tell me you're joking."

"I can't do that, Desi. I wouldn't joke about something so important"

"What about your promise to dad to finish your degree before leaving school?"

"I will keep that promise. I put together a good team. We are going to find the best sports agent available, so we can get the best deal possible and find a way for me to finish school."

Desi laughed so hard Neek thought she was losing her mind. "What's so funny about my news?"

"That shank pressured you to this for a long time. Now that you have made your mind up to do it, she's running around with that fool who's going to trade her out before she can say holdup. I know she doesn't know about your decision."

"You're sounding like Nell now. And no, she dumped me before I could share my good news with her."

A big smile crossed Desi's lips. "How is my man doing?"

"What did I tell you about that little girl?"

"I'm not a little girl. I'm working now and getting older every day."

"So is Nell. I told you to stop fantasizing about him. He is too old for you."

"He is just a few years older than me. Why do you and mama trip out about age so much?" Desi asked pouting her lips.

"Because we are trying to protect you from yourself. That is one of the main reasons I want to go pro. We need to get out of this neighborhood."

"Oh my God, I didn't think about that. We are going to be able to move. The best part is me and mama not going to have to work."

"Hold up, Desi. You may not have to work at a job, but you still going to have to work hard to get into a good college. You can also start taking your dance lessons again if you like."

Sadness crossed Desi's face. "Neek, I want to get out of this place, but I know how important it was to dad for you to finish your degree."

"You don't have to worry about that. I love school and will miss it, but I will not give up on getting my degree."

"It seems like all sports players do is practice off season. When will you have time to finish?"

"I'll make the time. Please don't tell anyone about my decision, especially X. I want to have a deal in place before I let too many people know."

"Scouts honor, big brother. I'm so excited. Everything is going to change. I can't wait to go shopping."

"Don't go spending money we haven't even gotten yet."

"Who are you going to sign with?"

"I have six teams that shown interest. I'm sure once I get a sports agent that number will increase. It has been my dream to be a Detroit Piston."

"Piston. Why not play for a team that can win a championship?"

"It's not all about winning, Desi. I have go get going. Remember no talking to anyone about this. Not even your girls."

"Okay, I heard you the first time. I love you, big brother."

"I love you too little sister." Neek gave his sister a brief hug and dragged her out of his room before leaving the house."

Chapter Six

Neek was exhausted. He couldn't believe Coach Rodgers had gathered so much information in such a short amount of time. Coach Rodgers explained deep down he knew Neek would choose to go pro after his last semester of school. Neek submitted his name for evaluation to the Undergraduate Advisory Committee (UAC). That was the first step before hiring a sports agent. Now they had to look for an agent that was National Basketball Players Association (NBPA) certified. Coach Rodgers sent Neek the names of the top three agents in the industry (one of which was located locally).

Coach Rodgers told Neek they were going to have to hurry to find him representation while they were waiting on a response from the UAC to let him know if he was going to be a part of the lottery draft. They knew this wasn't a problem with Neek's skills and reputation it would be shocking if he wasn't the number one pick. Within the file that was sent to Neek, the coach explained that what they needed to look out for in a sports agent which included cost, honesty, terms of the contract, reputation, and accessibility.

Neek knew from his research that a sports agent negotiated contracts and endorsement deals, assisted with financial planning, connected players with charity/public relations, provided career and legal advice, and counsel on relationship planning. He thought he had done through research but looking at what the coach sent to him he knew he was green in this area and was glad he selected a team of savvy people to help mold and build him for the present and the future.

The coach cautioned that until he is signed to a pro contract Neek had to be very careful not to fall into the bag many young players do when they first start out. They must make sure the agent will adhere to the only benefits that Neek can accept until he signs a deal are: transportation, lodging, and meals relating to meetings with the agent. Agents are not allowed to pay for training, nutritionist, or and other services provided by professionals.

Neek remembered the coach telling the team in one of their meetings that the main reason players need a contract is to have security and to let them know where they will be for the months/years to come. At the time they thought all this information was so boring they barely paid attention. Now that he was in the position where he needed this information he'd wished that he paid more attention. Especially when the coach was going on and on about the terms that should be in a contract like financial compensation, signing and incentive-based bonuses, the length of stay with the team, product/endorsements deals, and when and how the player will get paid.

Neek wanted to take a break from the report for a while. He had to make sure he looked over everything because he was going to meet with the coach in the morning. The coach wanted to go over some things before they met with the sports agent he had set up for early next week. This was finally getting real. Neek didn't know if he was ready, but he had to man up for himself and his family. Changing into his track clothes Neek decided to go for a run. He had to clear his head from all the millions of things that was floating around up there. He knew he should go to the university's gym to work out. He planned to start that schedule next week. He wanted to be as fit as possible.

Forgetting his water after he ran for three miles he stopped to catch his breath. Since he was near the neighborhood liquor store he ran over to see if the store manager would give him a bottle of water since he didn't have any money or id on him. As soon as he walked into the store he came face-to-face with the one person that had turned his life upside recently, Monica. It irked him that she looked fantastic with jewelry draped from her ears, neck, and hands. The clothes she was wearing were expensive.

"Hey, Monica, you're looking well this morning." Neek said.

"Hi, Neek, so do you." Monica said as she quickly tried to walk pass Neek.

"What's the rush?" You don't have time to talk to someone you were supposed to be deeply in love with less than a month ago?"

"I'm running late for an appointment. Please excuse me."

"So that is all you have to say to me, Monica?"

"Neek, I'm sorry, but as I said I'm late for an appointment." Monica rushed passed Neek and got into an expensive car he hadn't paid much attention to when he went into the store.

Once again Neek sat in Coach Rodgers office waiting on him to arrive. He still couldn't get over running into Monica earlier. He didn't like to say it, but she looked happy and content, although he knew she was nervous to see him for the first time since their breakup. Now knowing without a doubt, she was with that fool Ghost made him mad all over again. He was done with being hurt by her actions. The wounds that were slightly healing seemed to burst wide open. He forgot all about being thirsty and ran home a full speed. Having the house to himself was a blessing. He didn't feel like talking to anyone, especially his mom who would have I told you so written all over her face.

He started to call Nell but forgot he had an interview regarding an internship with an up and coming computer firm near downtown Detroit. After pouting for about an hour, Neek went to take a shower then gathered all the information he needed to meet with Coach Rodgers. Now that he sat there he was more determined to do his best to make sure he get everything he wanted from his decision to turn pro. He would work hard and wished to God, Monica would have the nerve to come crawling back to him, so he could tell her to go straight to hell. So deep into his thoughts he didn't hear the coach come in calling his name.

"Neek, what the hell is wrong with you? Didn't you hear me calling your name?"

"Sorry, Coach. I was thinking about running into Monica this morning. This was the first time I've seen her since she dumped me. She looked great."

"Neek, if you're serious about this turning pro thing you're going to have to put her out of your mind. You have a lot of hard work ahead of you."

"I know, Coach. I thought I was getting over her until I saw her again. I wanted to beg her to come back to me. When I was talking to Desi the other day, it didn't hurt as much. The way she was dressed and the car she was driving, I have to accept the fact she is now with Ghost."

"I know you're in pain, man but think about all the exciting things you're about to experience."

"Speaking of that, how in the world were you able to put all of this together so quickly?"

"I saw the look in your eyes when you finished last semester. I was praying my thoughts weren't correct but after our last conversation I knew I had to go ahead and do the best I could to take care of you."

"I appreciate that, Coach. I'm a little nervous about meeting with the agent next week. I need this more than ever now. I need something to keep me busy."

"You're going to be plenty busy for the next ten years or so." Coach Rodgers said with a smile on his face.

"Bring it on. I know I'm going to get a lot of flak because I truly want to be a Detroit Piston. That's is all me and my dad dreamed of since I was four years old."

"You're right. With the other high-powered teams showing interest it may be difficult to convince a sports agent your heart is here in Michigan."

"I have a responsibility to help my mom with Desi and X. I know I'm not going to have a lot of time to spare, but I don't want them to think I'm going to abandon them."

"Your mom and sister will understand, but your brother is a different story. Getting them into a better neighborhood and school system will go a long way."

"I know. I need to get Desi out of the hood. I don't want her to be Ghost's next victim."

"Don't take this the wrong way, Neek, but Monica isn't a victim. I know you still feel for her, but she had no loyalty for you."

"My head knows that but this heart of mine can't seem to let her go."

"Neek, I have another meeting shortly. Our next step before meeting with the agent is to sit down with your mom and sister to let them know what to expect."

"Okay, I'll set up something for tomorrow evening if that is good for you."

"Sure thing, I will see you all tomorrow. Not trying to exclude your little brother, but he is too you to understand."

"I got you, Coach. I will firm things up with you later today."

"Sounds good, Neek. Take care and I want to start seeing you in the gym every day." The coach and Neek laugh because they knew Neek should have been doing that all along whether he was turning pro or not.

Chapter Seven

Neek, Willa, or Desi didn't want the meeting with the coach to be held at their house, so they agreed to meet Coach Rodgers at the university in one of the conference rooms. They will have privacy because the building was almost completely empty except for the cleaning people. Willa was still upset with Neek that he was leaving school early and for having a closed mind about playing with the Pistons. She told Neek he should weigh all his options and not lock himself into a box. Desi was on her brother's side to support him and to piss her mom off. They still weren't getting along so she wanted Neek to stay close to home, so she could feel secure. The trio pasted big smiles on their faces when Coach Rodgers entered the room.

"Good evening, everyone. I hope you all day is going well so far." Coach Rodgers said.

"Hey, Coach Rodgers, you remember my mom and sister." Neek said.

"Sure, how are you guys doing, Mrs. Williamson, Desi."

"We're good. I told you to call me, Willa." Willa said.

"Sorry I forgot, Willa."

"Hey, Coach. Are you going to help my brother, so these fools won't take advantage of him?" Desi asked.

"Desi, watch our mouth." Willa scolded her daughter.

"I wasn't being disrespectful. I just know when you make a lot of money you have people coming out of nowhere to claim a piece of the pie. Plus, I don't want Neek to end up broke." Desiree explained.

"She's good, Willa. There is nothing wrong with her speaking her mind and looking out for her brother. In this business gathering the best support system could make a world of difference.

"I only told my mom and Desi that we have an appointment to meet with a sport agent on Tuesday." Neek spoke up.

"This is a very important meeting. We are a little behind the eight ball because the draft is approaching fast." Coach Rodgers said.

"Instead of rushing why not just wait until next year so Neek can have the time to do everything right." Willa asked.

"That would be idea, but since Neek has made his mind up to come out now that isn't an option. The ball is already in process. I understand where you are coming from Willa, but it is Neek's decision."

"Why can't you just back Neek up for once?" Desiree said to her mom.

"Desi watch your tone." Neek warned his sister.

"I'm not paying attention to that child's rants. I just want what's best for you and for you to have something to fall back on. After all, there is life after basketball." Willa said.

"Mama everything is going to work out. I love engineering. I will finish my degree and take care of all of us."

"I understand your concerns, Willa. That is why we're all have to work together to make sure we get Neek the best sports agent."

"Mama, I have put together a great support team. When we add the sports agent to the mix, everything will fall into place."

"When we do finally move, you need to make sure you don't let X's loser father know where we're living." Desi said with an attitude.

"I'm not going to tell you again to stay in your lane little girl. That's what's wrong with your little behind now. Going around here thinking you grown but behaving like a child." Willa replied.

"I asked you two not to start any mess while we were here. I'm sorry, Coach. I apologize for my family." Neek said.

Before Coach Rodgers could respond, Willa spoke up, "I have been doing some research since Neek is so dead set on doing this. I don't want my son to become a statistic."

"None of us want that, Willa. Neek has a great future ahead of him. If he had alerted me sooner of his decision we would be better off, but I know at least four teams that would be ecstatic to sign him."

"That's what I'm afraid of too. Neek needs to go wherever he can get the best deal. He is limiting himself by wanting to only play for the Pistons. His dad was wrong for drilling this into his head." Willa said.

"Mama, I don't want to play for the Pistons just for dad's sake. I've wanted to be a Piston all my life."

"What if another team makes a better offer? I don't want you to stay here so you can be close to us. You are already giving up too much."

"Mama, Neek is a grown man and should have a say as to where he wants to play. You may not need him around, but X and I do." Desi said.

"Stop being so damn selfish little girl. Between you and that gold digging tramp your brother had in his life he can't seem to catch a break dealing with selfish people."

"Coach, is there anything else you need to discuss right now. I need to get my family out of here. As you can see they don't know how to behave."

"That's enough for today. Please come together. Neek is going to have some tough times ahead. He is going to be pulled in several different directions. The last thing he needs to worry about is family members who refuse to try to get along."

"Listen, Coach Rodgers, I'm not trying to be difficult or make unfair demands on my brother. He wants to stay here and if the Pistons know what's good for them they will offer him the best contract to go along with his great skills."

"It's not always that simple, Desi. They have more than Neek to think about. They have to work around their budget and see the best way to align the team." Coach Rodgers explained.

"I don't know as much as you guys about basketball, but I do know Neek is the most sought-after college player right now. Any team would be blessed to have him. I love my brother and I want him to stay here but if he can get a better contact with another team and he wants to play for them, I will accept that." Desi said in a sad voice.

Neek went over to where Desi was sitting and gave her a big hug. "I want to be here for all of you and Nell. Ghost is really putting the pressure on him. He has Monica, but that isn't going to be enough to satisfy his need to hurt me. I don't want him coming after anyone else I love."

"We can work all of that out, big brother. When we move we don't have to let anyone know where we're at. We can also get security. I don't want you to worry about us. I know I've been out there, but I will take care of X when you're now around."

"I'm going to need you guys to take care of each other. Desi that means you have to be more respectfully to Mama." Neek said.

Looking over at her mom with a disgusted look on her face, Desi said, "She is going to have to do better as a mom. She let all of us down when Dad died. Granny died because she was so worried about her."

"I think you guys need to stay here for a little while and work this out. You're free to stay another couple of hours or so." Coach Rodgers said and left the conference room.

"Okay, Desi. It's time for you to fest up and tell us why you are so upset with Mom all the time."

Shooting an angry look at her mom, Desiree said, "Because she is weak. Granny tried her best to get her to act right, but she just ignored her."

"Desi, anyone can lose their way. I'm sorry you feel I let all of you down, but your Granny was a better grandmother than a mother." Willa said.

"See that is what I'm talking about. Even though she's dead, she still finds a way to blame everything on Granny."

"Desi, I love and miss Granny too, but we are a small family so we need to stick together. I don't want to be far away from you guys and have to worry about you all not getting along."

"I don't want that neither, Neek. I'm almost grown now. If she can be a better mother for X than we're good to go."

"It's disrespectful to call our mama, she. I know you're angry and that's why you've been acting out. Please try harder to be nicer to mama."

"Desi, I will try harder too. Once I don't have to work any longer I will get help with my issues and even take parenting classes if necessary." Willa promised.

"That's a big step. What do you say, Desi?" Neek asked.

"I will try too. Neek, I think I may need some help too. It may take a while for us to be comfortable around each other."

Before Neek could answer Coach Rodgers came back into the conference room. "Good news two more teams are interested in you, Neek. We're talking big time now, the Lakers and Warriors."

"That's great, Coach. We need to go home now. Thanks for doing this for us." Neek said.

"No problem. This is going to be a great journey for you, young man. Let's get out of here." Coach Rodgers walked the Williamson family to the front door entrance of the university and told Neek to be prepared for their meeting with the sports agent.

Chapter Eight

Neek and Nell arrived at the university a half hour before they were supposed to meet with Coach Rodgers and Pastor Nate. Neek was still angry at himself because he still missed Monica. He felt stupid because Monica had moved on with her life and didn't give him a second thought. Seeing her made things worse. He knew he couldn't compete with Ghost or anyone else with money until he turned pro. He thought Monica was down for him for the long haul. It turned out that she wanted to live the lifestyle where she didn't have to worry about money. Neek probably would have been able to get over Monica sooner if he hadn't seen her draped out in jewelry and driving that expensive car. Later he thought why she would come to the hood like that unless she wanted to run into him or the hood rats she wanted to get away from so desperately.

"Man, this shit is messed up. I hate that I can't get that heifer out of my mind." Neek said.

"Chill out, man. It hasn't been that long since you guys split."

"You mean since she dumped my ass like a hot potato." Neek corrected.

"Neek that is her lost. You need to stop tripping about something you can't change." Nell said.

"Now look who's talking. Wasn't it you just last year tripping when your girl called it quits and left town?"

"Yeah it was. I remember someone being in my ear telling me it's not the end of the world."

"Man, this is different. Monica and I had been down for almost three years while you and home girl were only together a hot second."

"The heart knows what it wants. We clicked faster than most couples. Besides, she was the aggressor."

"Hey, let's talk about something serious before we meet with the others."

"Oh no, I don't think I'm going to like this."

"All jokes aside, man. I was thinking about all the changes to me and my family when I turn pro and that includes you."

"Neek, I'm going to tell you again. Get the best deal possible wherever they are offering it. The NBA isn't a career. They will turn their backs on you in a split second if you get hurt or couldn't play for any other reason."

"I know all of that, but like you said the heart knows what it wants. I've dream of being in a Detroit Piston uniform forever."

"Man, they already have Reggie Jackson, Langston Galloway, and Jameer Nelson."

"I know, and they could have Domineek Williamson that can challenge any player for Rookie of the Year, young legs, and an intense knowledge of the game."

"Have a big head much?" Nell said with a smirk on his face.

"No, I'm just confident in my playing skills and knowledge of the game. Stop getting me off the subject. I know you want to finish your last year at the blue and gold, but how would you feel if plans change and you could transfer to another school or state?"

"Stop it, Dude. You're not going to use me to stick around here anymore than your family going to let you use them. I'm cool so just chill."

"What's wrong with me looking out for my family? You know any chance Ghost have of sticking it to me he will."

"Neek, I'm not some young naïve kid. I agree you need to get your family out of this hell hole ASAP but as far as I'm concern, there is no need to push the panic button."

"Nell, you're like a brother to me. All you have done to help me and my family I want to show my gratitude."

"You can by getting off your ass and getting the best contract possible. Plus, all I did was share time with you guys. We both know I don't have a penny to spare. Desi is becoming out of control, so you need to handle her right away."

"I know, man. The main reason I would sign a contract with another team is to get her as far away from the D as possible." Neek and Nell got out the car when they saw Coach Rodgers and Pastor Nate pull in.

The four men had been at it for over an hour now. Neek finally realized he may not be a Detroit Piston. He told the others that he would talk his mom into relocating if he didn't sign with the Pistons. This may be better for the whole family anyway. Neek didn't want to leave Nell behind, but he would make sure he was well taken care of so Nell wouldn't fall victim to Ghost's mind games. He wanted to get this meeting over with, so he could go talk to his mom and sister to see if he had to sign with another team besides the Pistons, will they be willing to relocate. Deciding they had covered enough Neek spoke up.

"So, to recap the qualifications of the sports agent should be his/her abilities to negotiate a contract; obtain endorsements; provide financial planning; relationship planning; career advice; and legal advisor."

"Basically yes, also a part of their job is to find new players. Some agents spend a good deal of time scouting new players." Coach Rodgers added.

"I know. I've been receiving quite a few calls over the last few years." I'm all about the numbers and don't plan on getting jibbed.

According to the research I gathered it seems that agents typically earns ten to twenty percent of a client's contracts and endorsements." Neek said.

"True, but some could go as high as twenty-five percent and be entitled to that percentage of the player's signing and Championship bonuses too. But since the Rookie contract is different they can't get a percentage of that because of the salary cap set by the CBA (Collective Bargaining Agreement)." Coach Rodgers explained.

"Wow, these guys are vultures." Nell added.

"They just doing their jobs. Since they usually don't get any upfront money they have to recoup for their time and expenses." Coach Rodgers said.

"So, you're saying they are locked out of the Rookie contract process?" Pastor Nate asked speaking up for the first time.

"Yes, that is pretty much the gist of it." Coach Rodgers said.

"Coach is there anything else we need to cover before tomorrow's meeting? I want to go talk to my mom and Desi about all of this and see if they will be willing to relocate if I don't get signed with the Pistons."

"No, I think we covered everything. Be ready to deal with some tough decisions tomorrow."

"Will do, Coach. I appreciate all of you taking the time to help me out. Enjoy the rest of your day." Neek and Nell left the men at the conference room table while they headed to his house.

Chapter Nine

The day had finally come. Neek and Coach Rodgers had just pulled into the parking lot of sports agent Davison Allen Greene firm DAG Sports Management (DAG). Davidson was a highly recommended agent for getting the best deals for rookie players. Neek was surprised Davie was able to meet with them on such short notice. At first Neek wanted to sign with an African American agent, but Coach Rodgers told him he needed to think about the best person to represent his career not the color of that person's skin. Davie's reputation preceded him as he has signed the last three number one draft picks out of the last four years. This impressed Neek because these players were still with their original teams and one was offered an extended contract.

Walking into the lobby, Neek felt an instant peace come over him. He didn't know if it was the baby blue and other bright colors of the reception area. Neek vaguely remember Davie reaching out to him in his sophomore year at U of D Mercy. He was nowhere near ready to think about leaving school, so he blew him off. It had become an irritation to him with all the agents coming at him about leaving school early. He just ignored them since he wasn't interested. They had even started to harass his mom. The receptionist at the front desk escort Neek and Coach Rodgers into Davie's waiting area and told them his assistant would be with them shortly.

The men sat down for a few minutes when a beautiful African American woman approached them announcing herself as Davie's assistant, Myra. She was tall for a woman nearly six feet slim with bright brown eyes. Escorting them into Davie's office and quickly leaving, the men didn't get much of a chance to communicate with her. A few minutes later Davie walked into the office. Neek immediately felt a connection with the former basketball player. He was a few inches taller than Neek. Neek knew Davidson would be his sports agent.

"Gentlemen, so glad you could make it. Would you like a snack or a drink? Help yourselves at the bar." Davidson said.

The men turned in the direction Davidson was pointing. This was the first time that they noticed the bar with assortments of drinks, fruit, cheeses, crackers, and pastries. Too nervous to eat, Neek and Coach Rodgers declined Davidson's offer.

"Let's get to know each other a little better. My name is Davidson Allen Greene. Please call me Davie. Davidson is a name I would rather forget. I love the game of basketball. My dream of becoming a pro player disintegrated when I busted my knee in my senior year at University of Michigan. I continued my education in sports medicine. After that I went on to get my Master's in Management. I became a sports agent fifteen years ago and have signed three of the last four first round draft picks. Neek tell me about you." Davie said with an interesting look on his face.

Not nervous at all anymore since Davie shared his information, Neek started. "Basketball has been a part of my life since I was four years old. My dad's dream was to see me wearing a Piston's jersey. He sacrificed a lot to get proper training for me. He is decease now. Running a close second to basketball is the importance of getting my engineering degree. My family consists of my mom, younger sister and brother, and my best friend Donnell who is like a brother to me."

"Interesting, usually when I ask this question players don't bring up their wanting to finish college. The thrill of joining the NBA is all that is on their mind." Davidson responded.

"It was a very tough decision for me to leave school early. I promised my dad that I wouldn't turn pro until I'd gotten my degree."

"You can still get your degree if you are willing to make sacrifices. It won't be easy but anything worth having in life isn't easy."

"I appreciate you saying that. I have a great support system. Coach Rodgers has been a Godsend. He has supported me even though he doesn't like my decision to leave school."

"What are your misgivings about Neek's decision, Coach?" Davie asked.

"Neek is a great player with drive and determination. He has surpassed plenty of obstacles to get where he is today. With his talent and skills, he will still be a great prospect a year from now after he has completed school." Coach Rodgers explained.

"That's true, but the sooner he gets signed the better deal he can get. The NBA is always looking for the next LeBron James or Michael Jordan." Davie added.

"I need this challenge in my life right now. I know the road ahead isn't going to be easy, but I'm ready. I don't see myself as cocky but confident." Neek explained.

"Alright let's move on. What brought you to my agency?"

"Even before Neek told me he wanted to turn pro, I decided it was time for me to do research on who would represent my guys once they were ready. I know since Neek is leaving other from the team would probably decide to cut their college program short. You were among the top three sports agents in the industry." Coach Rodgers said.

"I see you've done your homework, Coach. What else did you learn about me?"

"That you are registered with the state; you have never been disbarred; your fee is higher than most agents, but you get results; you take the time to make sure your athletes are prepared for the draft; that I could find you don't take kickback from referrals; your caseload is manageable; and you have great endorsements connections." Coach Rodgers listed.

Davie was impressed. He smiled slightly, "I see you are in good hands, Neek. Are there any questions you would like to ask me?"

"Yes, I have a few. To start with not meaning to get too personal or offend you, but I'm a by the number guy. How are your finances?" Neek asked.

"That's an astute question, Neek. I'm not having any financial difficulties. Not bragging, but over the last five years my business has been booming with bringing in the last three number one picks out of four years on board. By the way young man, no offence taken. You wouldn't have to worry about me putting my financial needs before your needs."

"Cool. That's another thing I wondered about. With so many high-profile players you are handling, how much time would you have to give me?"

"Neek you wouldn't have to worry about your pecking order. Yes, I have a high-profile clientele, but they are not high maintenance. So far, I've been blessed with not having to put out too many fires. If you sign on with me, I will have time to dedicate to building your career."

"I guess my last question would be, what is your damage control plan?" I don't drink, do drugs, or gamble, but I do come with the baggage of my parent's rocky relationship, my younger sister tenancy of going wild, and an ex-girlfriend who will do anything do get out of the hood."

"To be honest with you, Neek, I know about all of that and you have nothing I could find in your past that I couldn't spin. The first three years of your career something will probably go wrong. The only thing I'm truly concerned that will come back to bite you is the situation with your ex-girlfriend. When you're in the limelight there is a big possibility she will come running back to you. How will you handle that situation?"

Neek was silent for a few moments. His breakup from Monica was still a touchy subject. "I'm still raw about the situation, but she has no place in my life any longer. If she comes back I won't give her the time of day."

"Okay, the next thing we have to deal with and be realistic about is the first three years of a contact something can and most likely will go wrong such as demotion, released, injury, or playing for a horrible team/coach. This is when I can work my magic to protect you in situations like this."

"So, you are saying that you won't cut and run leaving me high and dry if one of those situations happened to me?"

"That's exactly what I'm saying. Most agents in the field will stop working if you get injured or cut from the team. With me that is when my job starts. I pride myself on making my athletes feel confident that I won't leave them when they go through a tough spell. It is still the agent's duty to make sure a player is taken care of medically and financially from the league, team, and state workers' comp."

"Coach, I think we covered everything unless you have something else you want to address." Neek said.

"No, not at this time. This has been an informative meeting. Where do you want to go from here, Davie?" Coach Rodgers asked.

"Over the next week or so, I will put together a mock contact that will contain what I can offer as an agent and what I expect from you, Neek. I need you to read it carefully, take time to get all your concerns addressed, and set up an appointment with me when you are ready to sign on the dotted line. If you decide you don't want to sign with me, I will ask that you send back to me via certified mail any documentation you received from me." Davie said.

"No problem. We will be in touch." Neek and Coach Rodgers stood and shook Davie's hand.

"I look forward to seeing you again, Neek. Make sure you stay in the gym. If you sign with me it will be mandatory to train six days a week."

"No problem, Davie."

"Myra will be more than happy to escort you gentlemen out." Davie walked back to his desk and made a vow to himself. He will get this kid signed no matter what he had to offer him. He could be bigger that Jordan and James.

Chapter Ten

The next morning Neek got up early to take a run to clear his head. Before he headed to the track he thought about the beat up used car he was driving. Imaging himself in a brand-new car and other material things were exciting. He tried not to let this go to his head, but he was ready for the improved lifestyle money will bring. It was hard for him to sleep last night because the meeting with Davie was fresh in his mind. He was a little worried about his mom's shady past being out there in public and the trouble Desi had gotten herself into when she was hanging out with the wrong crowd. His biggest concern was the trouble he had a feeling Monica would create once she found out he was going pro.

Neek wasn't a hundred percent sure he would be able to resist Monica if she tried to come back to him. He was still hurt by her dumping him, but he also still loved her. When he expressed in the meeting yesterday that his past with Monica wouldn't be a problem he meant it but dreaming about her last night made him realize he was still emotionally tied to her. His hopes were that once he started his busy schedule with the pre-draft process, he wouldn't have time to think about her so much. Neek sat on the first bench on the track field to think about when he was twelve and he was first introduced to the exciting field of engineering. He, Nell, and Ghost were in middle school when they had this job fair. Nell was already a computer geek while Ghost was always trying to figure out how to make a quick buck.

As the trio walked around to talk to the different people that came by to share their wares, Neek left the other two when he saw the layout for the structure of two new buildings planned for the metro Detroit area. The presenters provided such interesting information that Neek was still excited about all he learned and was happy to share it with his dad when he went to visit him the following weekend. He still remembered sharing with his dad what he wanted to do with his life besides basketball.

"Dad, I had a great week in school."

"Really, what was so great about it, Neek?"

"We had a job fair at the school. There were guys from different professions trying to convince us why their field of work was so important."

"Sounds good, Neek, what was the best presentation to you?"

"It was these two guys from the company that will be in charge for the buildings that are going up soon. They were engineers."

"Okay. I understand you were excited about the fair, but don't go getting any ideas in your head that will take away from your basketball training."

"But, Dad, you don't understand. They were telling me since I was good at numbers and figuring out how things should work, I would be an excellent candidate for their junior civil engineering program."

"Neek, you don't have time to start something new. We have all we could handle with your basketball training. When will you find the time to focus on something that sounds so demanding?"

"Dad, I'll make the time. Basketball is important to me, but I would love to see what the program will offer. Anyway, I can't join until I'll fourteen, but the guys said since I have potential they could show me the ropes."

"Neek we can talk about this later. Now let's go hit the hoop."

"Yes, sir, I'll be ready in a few minutes."

Neek remembered having his dreams dashed that day. He understood where his dad was coming from. JD had spent a lot of money and almost all his free time working with Neek to become a star basketball player. During the week when he wasn't with his dad and practicing, Neek kept in touch with the engineers and by the time he turned fourteen he was so happy that his dad had a change of heart and let him do the junior program the engineers offered. Deciding it was time to get back home, Neek got into his car with a few tears in his eyes thinking about his dad's reaction to his turning pro.

When Neek got back home from his run, X was up eating a bowl of cereal. He loved his little brother, but he didn't understand his fascination to cereal. X could eat cereal for breakfast, lunch, and dinner and still not be tired of eating it. Neek wondered where Desi was at. She was supposed to be watching their little brother instead of putting him in front of the TV. Neek didn't see where his mom and sister's relationship had improved since the meeting. They still walked around the house avoiding each other. He didn't want to think about his mom and sister right now, he wanted to focus on his little brother.

"What's up, X?"

"Hey, Neek, can we do something today, just the two of us?" X asked.

"What would you like to do, Little Man?"

"Neek, I thought you were going to stop calling me that. I'm not a kid anymore."

"My bag, what would you like to do today, X?"

"That's much better. Can we go to the carnival after I finish eating and cleaning my room?"

"It's hot out there. Wouldn't you rather go someplace on the inside?"

"No, I want to go to the carnival. I haven't been there since me, you, and your dad went there."

When X mentioned JD, Neek became sad all over again. His dad was hard on him, but he missed him like crazy. He remembered that day well. His dad didn't want to take X with them. When Willa had X, JD refused to talk to her or have anything to do with X. "Okay. Be ready in an hour. We need to go early before it gets too hot and crowded out."

"Thanks, Neek, I love you." X didn't bother to take his dish to the kitchen. He ran upstairs like a pack of pit bulls were chasing him.

"Make sure you brush your teeth." Neek yelled out as X ran up the stairs. Neek checked his pockets. It was saddening to only find fifty dollars. He guessed he could put the entry fee to the carnival on his credit card, but something had to give. He was so sick of not having enough money to do even the simple things in life.

Chapter Eleven

It was now Saturday morning. Almost a week had went by and Neek still hadn't heard from Davie. He wasn't worried because he could tell from the meeting that Davie was anxious to sign a deal with him. Neek sat in the same restaurant where Monica dumped him waiting on Nell to get there. At first, he didn't want to step foot back into that place, but to move on he knew he had to get over his hard feelings surrounding Monica. Neek waved his hand when he saw Nell walk through the door. He was going to miss hanging out with Nell when he started his training for the pre-draft. When Nell reached the table, he grabbed the chair across from Neek.

"Wow, man, you look like you had one too many last night." Neek said.

"Man, why the hell are you talking so loud?" Nell responded.

With a smile on his face Neek yelled, "This is loud." Before Nell could respond the waitress came over to take their order. They both ordered the breakfast special. Neek had water and orange juice while Nell ordered coffee.

They were almost done eating their meal when Neek looked up from his plate and saw a couple walk through the door. He knew he was going to run into them eventually, but he was still caught off guard. He wasn't going to let it show but he was taken aback. Nell wondered what had his best friend acting so strangely when he turned around to see Monica and Ghost head their way.

"This shit can't be happening right now." Neek said before the couple reached the table. Monica looked nervous while Ghost looked like he just hit the lottery.

"What's up fam?" Ghost said in a cheerful voice. This is how they used to greet each other when they were close.

"Good morning." That was all both Neek and Nell said.

"We're so glad to run into both of you on this bright and sunny morning. My bae and I would love for you guys to join us tonight for our engagement bash." Ghost said.

Neek was shocked but hoped it didn't show on his face. How could Monica move on so fast? "Sorry, I have plans already." That was all Neek could get out. He just wanted to get the hell out of there.

"You're on some real crazy shit if you think we would come to anything you give, Ghost." Nell said.

"Well, we better get going. We must make sure we eat well this morning, so we can enjoy our big night ahead. Turn up." Ghost and Monica went and sat in a private booth in the back of the restaurant. Not surprising, Monica didn't say one word.

"Neek, are you okay?" Nell asked.

"I'm good."

"You need to go off. It's not good to keep all this bottled up."

"I said I'm good. Let's get out of here." Neek grabbed the check and told Nell he would catch up with him later.

Neek was so glad when he returned home the house was empty. His mom was at work, Desi was out with her friends, and X was at a sleepover. He was barely able to make it home without wanting to hit something. He should have gone straight to the gym to work his frustrations out, but he didn't want to be around people. Locally he was already a famous basketball player. Sometimes he would get stop and asked when he was going to join the NBA. Going straight to his room and flopping down on his bed, he thought about what happened earlier.

It took all his will power not to beat the shit out of ghost. He knew he couldn't afford to get into an altercation. Plus, he knew that

Ghost's men were somewhere close by. Neek still couldn't fandom Monica being engaged, especially to Ghost. When they first started dating he remembered how much Monica claimed to dislike Ghost. She said he was rude and ghetto as hell. Now a few years later she was set to marry him. This was a slap in the face. He thought she was down for him. He wished he could stop caring about her low-down ass.

Seeing Monica with Ghost made Neek wonder where their relationship went wrong. Monica was so important to him because she was his first real love. He dated before and had casual arrangements with other women, but when he met Monica none of those other women was on his radar. That was one of the happiest days in his life. Neek went back down in memory lane to the first time he met Monica on the University of Detroit Mercy campus. Classes had started a few weeks back. Monica was a late enrollee because she didn't want to go to school again after dropping out of Wayne State, but her family forced her. The instructor asked the class to split into small groups. When Monica sat there like she was lost, the instructor asked Neek to let her join his group. Once class was over Neek stayed behind to talk to Monica.

"Don't be afraid of us, we're not going to bite you."

"Who said I'm afraid." Monica said quietly.

"I do. It looked like you were going to jump out of your skin when you were placed in our group."

"That's not true. I just don't like being a part of a group when my grade depends on what others do or don't do."

"You are fortunate to be placed in our group. We are the smartest group in the class."

"And this is coming from the person who walks around with different color socks on."

"Oh, you got jokes now. I'm making a statement."

"What's statement is that? That you are colorblind."

"No. That I'm my own person and I make the rules I want to follow."

"Whatever, I have to get out of here."

"See you next week. Make sure you are ready to dig into the project when we meet again." Neek remembered Monica rolling her eyes at him as she walked out the door.

Neek felt like a fool when he came back to the present and his face was wet. He prayed each morning and night for God to give him the strength to let Monica go. It should have been enough seeing her with Ghost and finding out they were engaged. It hurt even more because he could see that her entire personality had changed. She wasn't that outgoing person of her past. He laughed at himself because if Desi was there she would say that Monica was going through Glow-up. Neek didn't like that term, but it was exactly what was happening with Monica. Knowing that it was time to put Monica behind him Neek concentrated on training, getting an agent, and going to the draft.

Chapter Twelve

It was Monday morning. Neek didn't sleep well last night. The good thing was it wasn't because of Monica this time. The closer it came to Draft Day the more anxious he became. In his heart he knew his dad would forgive him because all he wanted to do was take care of his family. He heard Desi getting ready for her summer job. His mom had left more than an hour ago. X was playing the video game. He wished his little brother wasn't so focused on that game, but he was like so many kids his age. Neek thought before his schedule wouldn't permit, he was going to spend more time with X. His mom had enrolled X in the summer day care program because Desi couldn't watch him, and she didn't want Neek putting off something he had to do to babysit. The ringing of the doorbell had Neek charging down the stairs. It was UPS with a package for him. As he was about to close the door X's bus pulled up in front of the house. After seeing his brother off, Neek went into the kitchen to open his package.

Shouting YES to the top of his lungs, Neek was so happy to receive the mock contract from Davie. The next thing he did was call his support team and asked if they could meet as soon as possible to go over the contract. He was glad they were able to meet today. They agreed to meet at the church at one o'clock. Davie mentioned that he hoped he was ready to be sign with his agency and to schedule a meeting within the next few days in his cover letter. Neek glanced at the terms of the contract. Since he preferred to wait to meet with the others before going through the tons of paperwork, Neek decided to give his mind a rest and go back to his earlier days when he was forced to learn there was more to basketball then shooting and playing the game. His dad and the many basketball camps he attended taught him all about the game.

"Neek now that you are well versed on how to shoot and defend, you need to know the fundamentals of the game."

"Dad, I don't need to know about that stuff, that's what the coach in there for. I need to keep practicing on my shooting." Neek replied.

"No, son, you need to know the game to be a valuable player. It's good that you are confident with your skills, but what will keep you on the bench is ball hogging. You have a tenancy of doing that. It's not a good trait."

"But, Dad, if I'm the best baller the ball should be in my hands."

"Neek stop this foolishness right now. I know the camp or school didn't teach you this nonsense."

"Why is it nonsense, Dad? Ghost said that I need to be a take charge baller."

"What I tell you about listening to that thug?"

"Sorry, Dad, camp and coach told me about the importance of being a good ball handler. Passing the ball will keep me out of trouble with the coach and my teammates."

"That's what I like to hear, Neek. Now, you make sure you keep listening to the coach. The scouts are showing interest in you, but we can't take that for granted.

"I know, Dad. The coach said scouts go around to tons of schools looking for talent. That is why he is so hard on us to keep our grades up and be seen for more than just basketball."

"That's smart of you, son. Now let's get down to business."

Neek had a big smile on his face. He had so many mixed feelings about his dad. One thing was for sure he loved him, but he didn't like the way his dad walked out on them and the way he treated his mom. Neek felt that is the reason why his mom got involved with X's gangster father.

By the time Neek made it to the church everyone was already there. Neek was glad Nell was there to give a younger perspective and to keep him busy. Neek had no intentions of abandoning Nell once he turned pro. He knew Nell was going to be too proud to take anything from him once he started making money so he decided on drawing up a contract so he could loan Nell the money, so he wouldn't have to worry about how he would survive until he completed his degree. Neek had already discussed this with his mom.

The men met in the small conference room next to Pastor's Nate office. This was the room the trustee board used to count the money after church services. Neek tried to tell Nell he needed him to be part of this team when Nell brought up that he felt he didn't bring anything to the table. Since Nell was a computer geek Neek told Nell his job was going to be to make sure everything was kept in order. With contract negotiations, endorsements, public appearances, and charity functions, Neek didn't want anything to fall through the cracks. Plus, Nell had a sharp mind and was detailed oriented. Neek started the conversation off after Pastor Nate finished the opening prayer. He thought he was going to burst with excitement.

"This all seems so unreal to me at times. When I look and saw the contract I thought I was going to have a heart attack."

"Neek calm down, man, you can't let them know how anxious you are." Coach Rodgers said.

"I know, but it is so hard. I knew this was coming but for it to actually happen seems like an out of body experience."

"This is only the beginning. I know Davie tried to play it cool, but he wants to sign you badly. The other number one picks are slowly faded to the back burner. He knows he would have years of work if he signs you on." Coach Rodgers said.

Neek gave the package he received from Davie to Coach Rodgers. Coach Rodgers carefully took everything out of the package.

"Before we get started on this we need to bring Pastor Nate and Nell up to speed of what your life is about to become. When we leave here Neek we're heading over to the gym. Never take your eyes off the prize and always practice."

"Coach, I've been going over the many tips I've learned from my dad, basketball camps, high school basketball, and of course my years with you. I know there is always more to learn about the game."

"Coach Rodgers, I know a lot about what Neek have been though over the years with his training. I helped him to rehearse his tips, practice his balling skills, and pushed him when life came crashing down." Nell said.

"I'm glad to hear that, Nell. Every one of us at this table will bring something important into Neek's life. Pastor Nate, times will get hard for Neek. He is going to need your guidance and strength to get him through the tough times."

"My doors are always open for this young man. I must say it's good to be close to him. I miss JD but being involved with Neek's life gives me pleasure in knowing that his spirit stills lives on."

"The draft is less than a month away. If Neek is going to sign with Davie's agency the time is now. He would want Neek to start the pre-draft camps immediately. He would want to get Neek more exposure. This would help when pitching Neek to teams and getting him prime endorsements." Coach Rodgers explained.

"So, what you're saying is that Davie's job would be to promote Neek to get him a good placement in the draft?" Nell asked.

"That's correct. Neek, I know you've been working out and keeping in shape, but you have to now prepare yourself for the most grueling and intensive training you have ever encountered."

"I'm already physically and mentally prepared for that, Coach. Looking at pass drafts, I know my work is cut out for me. If I'm the number one pick all eyes would be on me. This is intimidating, but I'm going to keep my eyes on the bigger prize: securing my future and taking care of my family." Neek said.

"Okay. Let's see what we have here. I know from Davie's reputation. He isn't just looking to secure your rookie years. He would at the least aim for a four-year deal. He knows his hands are tied with the salary cap for the rookie contract but after that is when the negotiation really gets started."

"I've done a little research but refresh me on how the draft works." Pastor Nate asked.

"To sum it up a little since we don't have that much time, the draft consists of two thirty round picks. Each team would be allowed to pick in each round unless they have traded their picks for players, money, or future draft picks." Coach Rodgers explained.

"What are the figures Davie put in this mock contract, Coach?" Neek asked.

"Davie broke it down to the league's salary cap of six point eight million with a possibility for an additional one point three million if incentives are used."

"Wow, so you're saying that Neek can earn over eight million in his first year?" Nell asked.

"Roughly he could earn more than that with other incentives and bonuses. Davie's job is to get whatever team Neek signs with to offer him an extension on his rookie contract to keep him out of free agency." Coach Rodgers answered.

"This is really deep." Pastor Nate said.

Coach Rodgers reviewed the contract thoroughly before speaking again. "Most everything in this contract is pretty normal. It is broken down to what Davie will do for Neek outside of negotiating his contract. He added possible endorsement deals, financial planning structure, and what he could do to build Neek's reputation. The one thing I would like to get him to change is his percentage. He's asking for four percent of the playing contract and twenty percent of endorsements, meetings, and appearances

"So, he's asking for the highest possible percentages?" Neek asked.

"Seems that way, we need to make a counter offer." Coach Rodgers said.

"I'm thinking three percent of the player contract and fifteen percent of the others." Neek added.

"That sounds reasonable." Pastor Nate said.

"To us it may be. I don't think we will be able to get out of the four percent for the players contract, but we can definably bring him down on the others." Coach Rodgers said with a strange look on his face.

"What's up, Coach? You look like you just swallow something horrible?" Neek asked.

"I know this is a mock contract, but there is nothing in here stating that he will stick by you if your career takes a downward turn. I know he verbally mentioned that at our meeting but it's not here."

"Is there anything else missing, Coach?" Neek asked with a frown on his face.

"Everything else is straight forward."

"Okay. Let's do this. Arrange for a meeting with Davie within the next day or two. Nell, Pastor Nate would you guys like to be part of this meeting?" Neek asked.

"No, I think this is the part where you and Coach Rodgers shine." Pastor Nate said.

"I agree." Nell said.

"Cool. We can bring up the missing information issue when we meet with Davie. I think we all better get out of here." Neek said as they ended the meeting with a prayer by Pastor Nate.

Chapter Thirteen

Neek was exhausted. After the meeting with his support team he and Coach Rodgers headed to the gym where he worked out with Neek for the next four hours. By the time Neek arrived home he was so tired all he could muster up enough energy to do was call and make an appointment with Davie. He and Coach Rodgers were due to meet Davie on Wednesday at ten o'clock. Now that it was two hours before the meeting, Neek had to drag himself out of the bed so he could shower and get a bite to eat before leaving the house. It was so hard not to tell his family about the contract. Coach Rodgers told him he should wait until he officially signed with Davie before telling anyone outside of their support team.

Neek showered and headed downstairs to make some toast. That is about all his stomach could handle. After eating his toast and drinking two glasses of orange juice, Neek grabbed his gym bag and headed to Davie's office. He knew after the meeting he was going to have to work out extra hard since he didn't get up earlier to work out. When he arrived at DAG, Coach Rodgers pulled up behind him. Neek grabbed the Mock Contract and the men headed into the office. Once there Myra took them to a conference room where Davie was sitting at the head of the table. Myra went to the corner behind Davie to take notes.

"Good morning, gentlemen, so glad to see you again." Davie said in a loud and robust voice.

"Good morning, Davie." Neek said. Coach Rodgers just nodded at Davie. Neek glanced at Coach Rodgers and noticed a serious look on his face.

"I trust you all were able to review the contact." David said.

"Yes, we did." Neek answered.

"So, what do you think? Are we ready to talk business?" Davie asked.

Coach Rodgers nodded to Neek to take over. "Yes, most of the contract was acceptable outside of a few details."

"Since we are on time constraints with Draft Day less than a month away, what have you decided, Neek?" Davie asked as he leaned forward.

"My concerns were that you didn't state your commitment to me if something should go wrong in my career as we discussed at the previous meeting. Then there are the percentages."

"In the final contract my commitment to you will be addressed, this was just something for you to wrap your head around. As far as the percentage what are your concerns."

"I would like to come up with better figures that will be more agreeable."

"And what figures are more agreeable to you?"

"Three percent of the player's contract and fifteen percent of endorsements, meetings, and appearances would be a better fit."

Davie thought for a few minutes then with a big smile on his face he stood walked around the table and held out his hand. "You have a deal young man."

Neek couldn't believe his ears. He expected Davie to put up a big fight about the player's percentage. Neek glanced over at Coach Rodgers who slightly nodded his head. Neek stood and shook Davie's hand with a firm grip.

"So that's it. You are officially my agent." Neek asked.

"No, it's not official until we've sign on the dotted line." Davie said.

"When would that happen?" Neek asked.

"Come back tomorrow afternoon at one o'clock. I know its short notice, but I would like to take you and your family out for a celebration afterwards."

"Bet. I'll check with them to see what I can arrange. I would like for Coach Rodgers and Pastor Nate to come also."

"Sure, that's not a problem. I will need a headcount today, so reservations can be made. You will come in to sign the contract and we all can have a late lunch afterwards."

"Coach Rodgers will you be available for the signing and the celebration?" Neek asked.

"I should be able to arrange it. I know I can make it for the signing."

"Cool. We will see you tomorrow, Davie. I will get you that headcount later this afternoon." Neek shook hands again with Davie. After that he headed home to see if he could meet with his family to tell them the exciting news.

On his way home Neek called Nell to see if he could come over to his house in an hour. Nell said he would then Neek called Desi and asked her to make sure she came straight home after her summer job. Instead of waiting for X to come home from summer camp Neek went to pick him up before he headed home. His mom was the hardest to get to come home. She didn't want to cut her work hours short, but she agreed to be home in an hour. When Neek and X arrived home, Desi was already there with a million questions. Neek told her to chill out until the others arrived. Once the others arrived they all sat down at the dining room table.

"I've asked all of you here because you all are the most important people in my life. I love all of you very much." Neek said.

"Neek please tell me you are not getting back together with the trashy Monica." Desi said.

"No, Desi, this meeting doesn't have anything to do with Monica. I wanted you all here to let you know tomorrow I will be signing a contract with a sports agent. After the signing he wants to take us all out for a late lunch."

"Oh my God, it's finally happening. My big brother is going to the NBA." Desi said. She stood and went around the table to give Neek a big hug.

"Bet, man, you're on your way." Nell said.

"Mama, why aren't you saying anything, this is great news?" Neek asked.

"I'm happy for you, babe. I didn't think things would happen so quickly." Willa said.

Neek became concerned when he looked over at his little brother who sat quietly with tears rolling down his face. "X, are you okay?"

"Looking up at Neek, X said, "So I guess you're going to be leaving soon." X said.

"I don't have any of the details yet, but I told you wherever I go I want all of you to come too. My agent will know without a doubt that any deal I make would be in the best interest of all of us."

"Yes, we're going to be rich and I won't have to work at the stupid summer job any longer." Desi said.

"Girl, hush your mouth. You need to look at the bigger picture and not be concerned about how this will affect you." Willa scolded her daughter.

"Don't start on me. If you were in your right mind you would be happy how Neek's going pro will be the best for our family."

"You two need to cut it out. You can't behave like this tomorrow at the luncheon."

"I'm just sick of this girl being so selfish, Neek." Willa said.

"I know you're not calling me selfish when you ran off with a murderer. You need to look…" Desi didn't get a change to finish because Nell asked her to go outside with him.

After they were gone X said, "Desi is going to always hate my father, isn't she, Neek?"

"I wouldn't say hate. She is too young to realize some adult issues need to stay between the adults."

"This is the last time I'm going to let that girl bring up that man in front of my son. She needs to have more respect at least towards X who hasn't hurt anyone."

"I'll talk to her, Mama, but I'm serious. You guys can't embarrass me at the luncheon tomorrow. From here on out all of us must trend carefully. We can't do anything that will stop us from getting out of this horrible neighborhood."

"I hear you, babe. I better go and get dinner started." Willa gave both of her sons a slight kiss on their cheeks then headed to the kitchen.

"Neek, do you promise to take us with you? I don't' want to stay here without you." X asked sadly.

"I promise I will do my best to always have you guys close by me. Now let's go help Mama with dinner." Neek and X went to the kitchen. Neek hoped Nell was able to talk some sense into Desi.

Chapter Fourteen

Neek was wearing the better of his two suits the next day when he went to sign his contract with Davie. He confirmed with Davie yesterday there would be a total of seven at the luncheon. Pastor Nate was able to clear his calendar for the afternoon celebration. Like yesterday, Coach Rodgers was going to meet Neek at DAG. Neek talked to the coach for a few minutes last night to confirm he was going to be able to make it.

"Coach, you don't know how much I appreciate all that you are doing for me."

"It has been a pleasure working with you, Neek. Although I have mixed feelings about your decision, I wish you the best."

"Thanks for respecting my decision. I had to do what I felt was best for my family. Is this really going to happen tomorrow, Coach?"

"Yes, it is, Neek. You will need to keep your head on straight and stay close to your faith. The NBA is going to be tough and will challenge you. Remember to always keep your eyes on the prize."

"Thanks, Coach. I pray every day and night for God to give me the strength to stay on the right path. I'm realistic. I know there will be challenges coming at me from every direction."

"Okay, Neek. I will see you tomorrow. Be sure to dress your best for the signing."

"Sure thing, Coach, see you tomorrow." Neek showered and went to bed early.

Pulling up at DAG, Neek decided to wait in his car until the coach arrived. He wished Nell could have been there with them, but he didn't want to be involved in that part of the business. Neek had to respect that and be thankful for the support Nell has provided throughout their friendship. Neek felt more relaxed when Coach

Rodgers pulled in the parking spot next to him. The men got out the car and looked at each other with a big smile on their faces.

"Coach this still doesn't feel real. Am I about to sign on with an agent that will almost guarantee I'll be playing for the NBA in the fall?"

"Yes, Neek, this is it. We all are so proud of you. The next time you walk out of those doors, you will be one step closer to becoming a NBA player. Remember weigh all your options and don't settle. You are in the driver's seat. What you going to bring to the NBA will excite everyone involve."

"No use in putting this off. Let's go make this deal." Neek and Coach Rodgers headed into the building with high expectations.

On the other side of town Nell arrived at Neek's house to pick up Willa, Desi, and X. He was about to get out of his car when this bright red Lexus CT200h pulled up next to him. A grim look crossed his face when Monica exited the car. She was the last person he wanted to see on this special day. She was dressed in an expensive outfit like she was when she and Ghost ran into them at the restaurant. Even though she was a beautiful woman, Nell felt nothing for her but loathing.

"Girl if you don't get your trader ass from over here…" Nell was saying before Monica cut him off.

"Is it true? Is Neek leaving school to join the NBA?"

"I told you to leave right now, Monica."

"Answer my damn question, Nell." Monica persisted.

"That's none of your damn business. Now leave."

"I don't know where you get off trying to tell me what to do with your sorry looking broke ass."

"Listen, girl, get your ass out of here and go back to that savage that's going to end up pimping your stupid ass out."

Monica made a move to advance towards Nell when Desi came out of the house. She looked gorgeous in an Indigo blue dress with matching four-inch heels. Her hair was down for once with large soft curls flowing down her back. She wasn't happy at all when she saw Nell talking to Monica.

"I know you don't have the nerve to bring your tramp ass to my house." Desi yelled at Monica.

"I see my question is answered. This little twit is dressed for something." Monica said.

"That's it." Desi took her earrings off and was about to unstrap her shoes when another car pulled up in front of Monica's.

Ghost jumped out the car and headed straight for Monica. "What the hell are you doing over here?" Ghost asked Monica.

Before Monica could answer Desi did. "About to get the shit beat out her." Nell moved over to stand by Desi before she could finish taking her shoes off.

"You better go sit your young ass down, girl. Nobody got time to play your little games." Monica said to Desi.

"Man, you need to get your property and get the hell out of here." Nell said to Ghost.

"Stay out of this, dude." Ghost said.

"Ghost why are you here?" Monica asked.

"No, the better question is why your ass is here?" Ghost replied.

"Let's go. We can talk about this later." Monica responded.

"You bet your sweet ass we will." Ghost waited until Monica got in her car and pulled off. Then he gave Nell and Desi an evil glance before leaving without saying one word to them.

"What the hell was that about, Nell?" Desi asked.

"That trick found out about Neek's decision to join the NBA."

"That doesn't have shit to do with her sorry ass."

"We knew she would be sniffing at Nell once she found out about his decision."

"But to have the nerve to show up here was stupid on her part. Ghost is going to tear into her ass."

"Watch your mouth, Desi. Go get your mom and brother so we won't be late."

"Well, she needs to leave my brother alone. I'm not going to give her the chance to hurt him again." Desi left Nell to go tell the rest of her family it was time for them to leave.

Chapter Fifteen

The luncheon was held at SLOWS BAR BQ a popular cozy restaurant located in downtown Detroit on Michigan Ave. Known for its slow cuts meats and hearty sides SLOWS was also featured on cable TV and in numerous national and local publications. Everyone was seated in a private section located in the back of the restaurant. Neek was proud that so far, his family was on their best behavior and was dressed nicely. Desi looked like a young supermodel while his mom and baby brother was dressed in their best Sunday outfits. They had ordered their drinks and appetizers and was waiting on their entrees to be served.

"Before our food arrives, I want to thank everyone that is important in my life for being here today." Neek said.

"I would like to thank you all too. I hope to be a big part of this young man's life. He is on the road to become the most highly anticipated player since LeBron James. Not to mention that he is already an astute businessman. He's gotten more out of me that I expected" Davie said with a smile in his tone.

"Mama, why are you crying?" X asked.

Embarrassed that the attention was focused on her now, Willa said. "These are happy tears, baby boy. I'm just so proud of your brother and wished his dad was here to see what a great young man he turned out to be."

"No worries, Willa. JD is here with us and he is so proud of all of you." Pastor Nate said.

"I know he is. He would be the first to say that, Neek you are the greatest." Willa added.

"Before our food arrives, I would like to give you an overview of what will happen after today. I will start contacting team owners, managers and other individuals to get the best deal for Neek and to get endorsement deals on the professional side. On the personal side, I will work with Neek on financial planning, building relationships with the right people and guild his career."

"Speaking of all of that I know my son has his heart set on becoming a Piston. I have advised him to go with the team that will offer him the best deal. What are your plans to accomplish that goal?" Willa asked Davie.

"Willa, the Piston's along with several other teams are greatly interested in Neek. I will present the deals to him, but in the end, it will be his choice where he signs."

"Mama, I told you this is my greatest wish, but I will look out for all of us and make the best decision I can for my family."

"No, Neek. I told you that you need to make the best decisions that will benefit you. Your sister and brother are my responsibility not yours."

"Okay, Mama. We can talk about this later. Next, I want to present a few tokens of my appreciation." Neek reached in his briefcase that was sitting beside him. He removed four envelopes and past them out to Willa, Desi, X, and Nell. "To my family, I want you guys to know this is an open invitation for you all to come with me on this journey wherever it may take me. No matter where I end up playing, you guys are always welcome to come along."

Nell stood and gave Neek a brotherly hug. "Thanks, man."

"No thanks needed. You and X are the best brothers a person could have. Next I will like to thank Pastor Nate." Neek took out a nicely frame picture of Pastor Nate and JD from their earlier years. "You have been a rock for my family. I don't know what we would have done without your positive influence in our lives. Along with this I promise to make a sizable donation to First Baptist as soon as possible."

Pastor Nate stood and looked down at Neek's present. He couldn't believe Neek's kind gesture.

"Neek, I've watched you grow up from a child to a man. Like your mama said, JD would be so proud of you. You all meant the world to him." Pastor Nate said.

"I know my dad loved us. I just hope he will forgive me for not keeping my promise to him." Neek said sadly.

"JD was a reasonable man. He knows that some promises are broken out of necessity." Pastor Nate glanced at Willa's face that was now fully covered with tears.

"Last, but not least, Coach Rodgers. With your direction I have become a great basketball player. When I started U of D Mercy I thought I knew everything I needed to know about basketball. My dad, basketball camps, and high school coaches taught me the fundamentals. What you taught me that being a great shooter and ball handler is only the beginning. Under your supervision I learnt how to be a team player and play reader. I'm so blessed to have you in my corner." Neek reached in his briefcase again and pulled out an enlarged check with no amount, but it was signed with notes stating donation for U of D Sports Team.

Coach Rodgers looked at Neek smiling and shaking his head. He was really going to miss having Neek around. "You are so full of surprises, Neek. I knew when you joined my team that you were arrogant and misguided, but a talent second to none. Watching you improve over the years and growing mentally and spiritually made me realized that you are more than ready to take on the NBA. My misgiving at the beginning has been relieved. In its place knowing that there will be a gap on our team that will be impossible to replace is something I have to deal with."

"Young, man. I knew that there was a reason to sign you besides your remarkable talent. I now know you are going to outshine everyone and be the poster child for what determination and dedication will do for a person no matter what walk in life he/she comes from."

"Thanks, Davie. I look forward to having a long and blessed career with you and your firm." Neek said.

"It was so good to meet all of you. Please remember this day and continue to give Neek the support he's going to need. He is about to embark on an adventure that will elevate him to the next level. I must leave but please stay as long as you all like. There is an open tab to order whatever you like, and everything is taken care of. Neek, I will see you bright and early in the morning. Make sure you get some rest."

"Sure thing, Davie, I'll walk out with you." Neek and Davie left.

"Willa, this kid of yours is amazing, he has such a big heart." Pastor Nate said.

"I know. I'm just so glad that I was able to turn my life around. I hope my shady past doesn't come back to hurt my son's future." Willa replied.

"You don't have to worry about that, Willa. Davie has that all under control. He did an extensive background check on Neek long before he approached him in Neek's sophomore year at U of D." Coach Rodgers said.

"That's good. The last thing I need to do is to drag my son down when his career hasn't even taken off yet."

"Davie has only one concern that may present a problem for Neek, his past relationship with Monica." Coach Rodgers said.

This statement made Desi speak up. "That shank is going to be a problem. She had the nerve to bring her no good behind to our house today."

Neek returned just in time to hear what Desi said. "Monica came over today? What did she want?" Neek asked with an anxious look on his face.

"Man, forget about her. She is old news." Nell said.

"I said what did Monica want?" Neek repeated.

Glancing at all the people around the table before answering, Nell said, "She wanted to know if the rumors were true about you going to the NBA."

Neek sat down with an unexplainable look on his face. "Neek, we talked about this and you knew this may happen. Don't let this eat away at you." Coach Rodgers said.

"I won't. Let's order our food." The luncheon went on and everyone ended up having a good time.

Chapter Sixteen

Neek sat in Davie's office waiting on him to join him He felt good this morning even though he didn't sleep well last night. No matter how much he tried he couldn't get over the fact that Monica came over his house yesterday. He knew in his head that he needed to let her go but in his heart that was a hard thing to do. When he got home last night he stayed outside with Nell for a little while after the others went in. He needed all the details of what happened when Monica stopped by.

"Ok, what the hell happened with Monica earlier?" Neek asked his best friend.

"Man, that is one messed up chick. As soon as I pulled up to pick up the fam she brought her ass over here demanding to know if you were about to go pro." Nell explained.

"What did you tell her?"

"Everything happened so fast. We were out here talking when Desi came out. You can imagine how that went over."

"Okay, what happened next?"

"Well, Monica started in on Desi. Desi was in the process of taking her earrings and shoes off when that fool Ghost pulled up."

"What. You didn't say that Ghost was here too."

"We were celebrating something special. There was no need to bring everyone down. Anyway, Ghost pulled up and asked Monica what the hell she was doing over here."

"That's strange. He just pulled up out of the blue. He hasn't lowered himself to come back to this neighborhood for years." Neek said confused by Ghost's actions.

"No, it isn't. You know he just sees Monica as a piece of property he owns. He probably has a tracking device on her car or phone or both because she wasn't here a good ten minutes before he showed up."

"I knew this was going to happened. She is in way over her head. She is about to learn the hard way that Ghost is bad news."

"Man, that isn't your concern any longer. Monica made her choice and you need to make yours."

"I know I just hate to see her throw her life away."

"She has been throwing shade against you for a while now. Let her live with her bad choices."

"Peace, man. I need to turn in, so I can get an early start in the morning. Davie wants to do a full-blown bliss since we are kind of getting a late start." Neek showered and went to bed as soon as Nell left.

Neek came back to the present when he heard Davie enter his office. He felt guilty about not working out before their meeting.

"Neek it's so good to see you. I hope you all enjoyed your celebration yesterday"

"We sure did. The family is really excited about all of this."

"Good to hear. Now it's time to play catch up."

"Okay. What's happens next?"

"I'm looking to get you signed with a shoe company. I've made a pitch with a few of them to see which will offer the best deal. What I'm looking for is to sign a multi-million-dollar long-term contract."

"You think you will be able to do that. I thought those companies would only do contracts for rookie season."

"That's depends on the savvy of the agent. A good agent would get you endorsements well pass your rookie years."

"So, what you are saying is this deal will be in addition to the salary earned from signing with a team."

"Yes, and that is only the beginning. I'm looking to make you a multi-millionaire before you even play one game in the NBA."

"Wow, all of this is mind blowing. I knew there was big money in the NBA, but I didn't expect to make so much before the draft or signing with a team."

"Ok, I've digressed a little. We need to talk about what first round draft pick really means. We both know that you're going to be number one even though it will not be cemented until Draft Day. With the base pay under the rookie contract wage scale we're looking at roughly forty million with around eighteen million guaranteed for the first two years."

"Fierce. These numbers are amazing."

"For the first two years we are kind of pushed into a pigeon hole with the CBA (Collective Basketball Association). They have a tight grip on limiting the scale on what rookies should make."

"Yeah I've read up on them. At one point I wondered if I would need an agent for my rookie years since there is a cap on what can be paid."

"Well, I know it sounds self-serving, but I'm glad you decided to bring me on. Without an agent you may have been stuck with just the base pay. A good agent would be able to get you as much as one-hundred twenty percent of that base."

"So, you're saying that you're going to do that for me?"

"That and so much more, I'm going to ensure whatever team picks you up will add the incentive for third and fourth years."

"Wow, you're making this sound so easy."

"No, it won't be easy at all. Most of the teams even the better record teams are under budget constraints so they're going to want to suck you in by offering you the least as possible. My job will be to push them to their limits."

"As I mentioned yesterday during our contract meeting, you're taking a big risk on me. I know you're going to have to spend money on me that you may not be reimbursed."

"I've been in this business a long time. I know a great deal when I see it. I'm a businessman, but I care about all my clients. I know I will have to spend up-front money on you regarding housing, travel, transportation, gas, groceries, and other living expenses such as training and development, but I will get a return on my investment."

"Speaking of all of that, I'm still uncomfortable letting you take care of all of my expenses."

"That's a part of my job, Neek."

"But you're not getting any pay from my rookie contract."

"No, I'm not. But the three percent I will get from your second contract will more than compensate what I invested. I think we have gone over enough today. Stop by Myra's desk to pick up your itinerary for this week. Your pre-draft schedule will start tomorrow. You have my personal number. Feel free to use it if you have any questions or concerns. My doors are open twenty-four seven for you."

"Thanks, Davie, I'll check back in soon." When Neek left Davie's office he realized he was going to be a rich man soon.

Chapter Seventeen

It had been over a week since Neek started his new scheduled with Davie. So much had happened since then. Davie had Neek on a strenuous workout schedule. He scheduled Neek with a nutritionist to plan healthy eating habits and lifestyle. This was hard on Neek because he was used to eating at fast foods. Neek knew he had to change his mindset too. So, used to not having money he didn't know that he could eat out at fancier cafes and restaurants and still stay within a nutritious guideline. He waited a few days after meeting with Davie to tell his family about the windfall of making big money before the draft. He remembered the conversation fondly and that Willa, Desi, X, and Nell was left speechless. They were sitting at the dining room table where they usually met to have family discussions.

"Mama, I think it's time for you to turn in your notices at your jobs. I met with Davie a few days ago. He has a few deals in the works that would bring in big money before the draft."

"Neek, I can't just quit my jobs without any money saved." Willa protested.

"Didn't you hear what I just said? Our money worries are about to be over."

"Yes, does that mean I can quit my summer job, Neek?" Desi asked in excitement.

"Yes, Desi, we all need to get our heads wrapped around living a better lifestyle. If you are ready, Desi to go take your road test. When the time comes I'm not going to buy you anything expensive, but it is time you had your own car, with the stipulation that you drive X to his day camp and other activities."

"Bet. That will still give me plenty of time to myself."

"Do you think she is mature enough for a car, Neek?" Willa asked.

"Mama, we have to give Desi a chance to grow up. I know she has made mistakes, but that comes with youth. The only thing I'm uncertain about is moving. We must get out of the hood. It wouldn't make sense for us to buy or rent a house since we are unsure if we would have to relocate."

"So, this is really happening. We are going to move and don't have to worry about money any longer." Willa finally realized they were going to have a better life.

"Nell, man what's up? I hope you will join us at our new place. I know you don't want to leave school. Another option you could get an apartment in a better area near the university." Neek suggested.

"It's a lot to take in. I didn't realize you would be making any money before the draft. You're right I do want to finish my last year at U of M. Getting an apartment closer to the school would be great."

"Cool, man. Not to come on too strong but we both need reliable cars. Let's plan to shop around in the next day or two to have something in mind when the money is in place."

"Come on, Neek. I don't want you buying me a car too." Nell said.

"You too, Mama, I know your car have sentimental value to you, but it's time for something new so I don't have to worry about you breaking down out there."

"Neek, I prefer to get my car fixed so it won't break down. I don't want anything flashy."

"Mama it doesn't have to be flashy, but it does need to be reliable."

"What about me. Since everyone is getting cars will I get me a new bike?" X asked.

"Sure, once we move in a better neighborhood. I'm not going to get you something nice, *X." Neek told his little brother.*

"Thanks, Neek. I'm going to check online to see what I want." X ran upstairs before anyone could say another word.

"Are we all on the same page? It's hard for me too, but it's time we start thinking like people with no money problems. Nell you're my brother in every sense of the word. Please don't let your pride stop you from a better life. Desi, I don't want you to go overboard. Yes, we're going to have money, but we have to keep it in perspective."

"I understand that, Neek, but we're going to have to dress the part of having real money. I just can't wait to leave the hood."

"Let's table this conversation for now. Mama, I'm serious. Turn in your notices. Davie expects big things to happen for us very soon.

Back to the present Neek had to meet with Davie in a few days to decide which company brand they will choose. He said they had three deal offers from Nike, Adidas, and Puma. Neek had to do some research with the other two companies because he has only worn Nike shoes. He remembered his dad always saying *the better the shoe the better your game would be*. Since his dad thought Nike was the best brand out, Neek didn't see any reason to change. With every new step he takes, Neek wished his dad was there physically to see that everything he sacrificed for him was finally paying off.

It took Coach Rodgers to explain to Neek why the companies were willing to pay him so much money before Draft Day. He told Neek that companies were eager for athletes to promote their products because it would draw in more customers. He also said that most of the endorsements contracts outlast the player's contract. The coach further explained that if great sponsorship decisions are made an athlete would never have to work another day in his life.

Neek did his own research about the products all three companies produced. He knew that shirts, hats, jackets, and socks were also products companies would want the athlete to endorse, but the shoes were the main product that was on the forefront of the deal. He learned a long time ago about the importance of good basketball shoes. The shoes would have to be able to grip the floor to allow quick cuts and crossovers. The shoe also should provide impact protection, so it could reduce the stress on the player's knees and feet. They should also provide support and protect the player's ankles from rolling.

When Neek thought about all that goes into basketball he now knew why many athletes fail. Most kids including him when he was growing up thought if you knew how to ball then that would be your ticket into the NBA. Now that he has researched, build up a dynamic support team, and hire Davie he felt he was better equipped than those who was not as grounded as he. Since he hadn't had much free time since starting his new schedule, but now had a twelve-hour opening, he decided to see what Nell was up to.

Chapter Eighteen

The day had finally come. Neek, Coach Rodgers, and Davie sat in DAG's conference room going over the three offers from Nike, Adidas, and Puma. The men had been reviewing the proposals for nearly an hour now. Neek still felt Nike was his best bet although the other brands offer a little bit more financially. He wanted Coach Rodgers to sit in because he was knowledgeable of today's trends and Neek felt more comfortable with him being there when making life changing decisions. Later that afternoon, Neek had an appointment with Pastor Nate. All of this was happening so fast he needed to get his mind back on track. Neek started the conversation after the men were done reviewing the proposals.

"This is a lot of information to soak up. I can't believe these offers." Neek said

"Hold your horses, Neek. I haven't shown you the latest figures from the brands since last week. These just became available to me yesterday." Davie said.

"So, you're saying they are trying to lower their offers?" Neek asked.

"See for yourself." Davie gave Neek and Coach Rodgers a booklet that contained the new offers with the bottom lines listed on the last page. Since the new proposals wasn't that long it only took Neek and Coach Rodgers ten minutes to review them.

"This can't be real. I feel like I'm dreaming." Neek said.

"It's real, Neek." Coach Rodgers said.

"The revised proposals came with your insane popularity on social media." Davie explained.

"But I'm not on social media." Neek said.

"You are now. I've have a team that is managing your Facebook, Twitter, and Instagram accounts. You have a few million followers."

"So, the revisions in the proposals happened because of social media presence?" Neek asked.

"Yes. Now that you are out there, Neek we're going to have to let the media meet the man behind Domineek Kane Williamson." Davie responded.

"What are you talking about, Davie?"

"After we sign with a brand we're going to have to start doing interviewing, guest appearances, and so forth. Most of this you will be doing individually, but on rare occasions your family and support team will be part of the process."

"Wow, I don't know if my family is ready for all of this. Just talking to them about moving and getting used to having money was a big change."

"No worries about that. I have a team of people that will work with them to make sure everything goes as it should."

"Coach, how do you feel about being a part of all of this?" Neek asked.

Taking his time before he spoke Coach Rodgers said, "I'm okay with it as long as we can work around my schedule. I don't' want the team to feel like I have less time for them because of your decision to go pro."

"Don't worry about that Coach Rodgers. My team can work around your schedule." Davie assured.

"Now, Neek, let's get back to the reason you're here. What brand do you want to accept?"

"I think we should go with Nike's offer." Neek responded.

"May I ask why?" Davie said.

"Not for the reason you think. I've always sported Nike. It's a great shoe. It gives me the use of the fast-all-angle attack because of its curved shaped of the outsole. It also allows me to respond with a rapid return of energy. It doesn't hurt that my dad thought it was the best shoe for sports. Plus, Nike offer will give more visibility. They are successful in standing behind their athletes and their contract offered longer terms."

"This kid is amazing. What brand to you feel Neek should go with, Coach Rodgers?" Davie asked.

I agree with, Neek. Nike's offer is the best. Plus, their shoes give the player the ability to fire the ball at all different angels of attack with its cushioning inside support."

"Okay. Let's say we go with Nike. The next bliss we're going to have to tackle is your charitable side. We need to make public what you have already done for U of D and First Baptist."

"Hold on a second, Davie. That was a private moment with my family and support team. It's not something I want to use to get attention." Neek protested.

"Neek your life is going to be an open book now. Your status will have people dissecting every part of your life."

"I realize I have to deal with the press eventually, but Draft Day hasn't even started yet. Damn I'm not running for public office."

"This is just the beginning. We have talked about this before. Your life will be open for the public to scrutinize. Remember we're building your brand that going to take you well into your career and retirement"

"Neek, it's not as bad as it seems. Personally, you have many things working in your favor such as: your ball skills, faith, commitment, and compassion." Coach Rodgers said.

"On the other hand, some of this can work against you. We have to be realistic. You must have tough skin in order survive in any sport now days. The media is just itching to dig up dirt to use against you." Davie added.

"Understood, so how long do I have to prepare my family for their interview?"

"I will set up something and let you know but expect it to happen between the next week. We also have to get them ready for Draft Day."

"Thanks, guys. If there is nothing else to go over right now I better head home." Neek said.

"One more thing, Neek, your home address has to change."

"I know, Davie, but until funds start to come in we are stuck in the hood."

"No worries about that, Neek. Start looking for something is a better neighborhood. I suggest Novi, West Bloomfield, or Troy. Once you are signed with Nike the money will start rolling in. You also need to get use to wearing their other products. I've notice you only sport the shoes."

"Like I said funds are tight. The extra money me and my mom have go towards activities for my siblings."

"I will get in touch with Nike today to get the ball rolling. Money won't be a problem after that." Davie assured.

"Good looking, Davie, hope to hear from you soon." After going over a few more details Neek and Coach Rodgers left Davie's office and went their respective ways.

<u>Chapter Nineteen</u>

Later that evening, Neek had dinner with his family at home. He ran around most of the day looking for a place for them to move. Searching in the cities Davie suggested was an eye opener. He knew living in the suburbs would be expensive, but damn they wanted an arm, leg, and heart for these places. He didn't look at any houses because not knowing what team he would be signing with it was hard to look for something permanent. He checked on condos, townhouses, and spacious apartments. After doing that he tried to catch up with Nell, but he was busy with one of his honeys.

Neek told his family he needed to talk to them after they finished dinner. Willa and X cleaned up after they were done while Desi said she had to check on some classes she wanted to take. The family knew she just wanted to get out of cleaning, but sometimes it was better to let her have her way than to argue with her. They decided to talk in the living room when everyone was ready.

"Mama, have you turned your notices in at work yet?" Neek asked.

"Yes, I did, Neek, Friday is my last day at my night job and I have another week at the day job." Willa replied.

"What about you, Desi?" Neek asked.

"I'm done. I was so glad to quit that job. I told them right away that I wouldn't be back."

"Good. I need to talk to you guys about my meeting with Davie and Coach Rodgers today."

"How is fine Coach Rodgers doing?" Desi asked knowing it would get under Neek's skin.

"Cut it out, Desi." Willa scolded her daughter.

"I'm just joking. That man is wayyyyy too old for me."

"By the end of this week I may be signing a deal with Nike." Neek said to his family.

"That soon, I thought it would take weeks for that to happen." Willa said.

"I didn't expect for it to happen this soon either. We have a lot to take care of in a short amount of time. After my meeting I got some listings for townhouses, condos, and apartment. Davie said we going to have to move soon."

"Neek we don't have money saved to move." Willa said concerned.

"Mama, the deal I sign with Nike is a multi-million dollars deal."

"Wow, we're going to be millionaires?" X spoke for the first time.

"Yes, X. We are going to be millionaires." Neek answered his little brother.

"I can't wait. Are we going to have a maid too? With our status change it wouldn't look right to be cleaning our own house." Desi said.

"Desi, we can work on that when the time comes. Now on to another subject, we're going to have to watch every move we make and not get into any trouble. The press will be all over us once this deal is signed."

"I don't like the sound of this, Neek. Between me and your sister we can be your downfall." Willa said.

"Oh no, you don't mix me in with your destructive behavior, Mama. My mistakes were nowhere near the dumb choices you've made."

"Desi, your attitude is going to have to change right now. You are no longer allowed to disrespect our mama." Neek said sternly.

"Why are you taking her side, Neek? She has hurt you more than the rest of us." Desi said pouting.

"That's in the past, Desi. We can't change anything that happened in the past. We just have to make sure we don't make the same mistakes again." Neek said.

"Yeah, Desi, you need to stop being so mean to Mama." X said.

"Why is this all about me. She is mean to me too, but she treats the two of you like gold." Desi complained.

"Desi, I'm sorry for hurting all of you. I told you we should go into counseling to work on our issues." Willa said.

"I'm not crazy so I'm not going to a shrink. It would be good for you to go." Desi said rolling her eyes at Willa.

"Let's table this for now. Davie is going to set up some interviews, guest appearances, and other things where sometimes you all are going to have to take a part in. I know for sure you all are going to have to attend Draft Day. He going to have his staff to work with all of us on how to answer the many questions that will be thrown our way."

"Wow, they should have given us more notice. I need to get my hair and nails done. I'll need a facial too, because I need to look my best. Who knows I may be the next start in the family." Desi said.

"Good Lord, Desi, why do you have to be so selfish? This is Neek turn to shine not yours." Willa said.

"I'm not trying to outshine Neek. All of us have to look our best right, Neek?"

"Yes, but you don't have to worry about that because Davie will have all of that taken care of. I just need you guys to behave and not embarrass the family when the time comes."

"I'll be good, Neek, but I'm scared I may say the wrong thing when they start asking us questions." X said.

"You don't have to worry about that, X. I told you there will be people working with us to prepare us all for how to answer any questions that is thrown our way."

"I'm glad, Neek, because I don't want to mess up and they take all of your money away." X continued.

"Thank you all for your support. We need to start packing. Don't worry about clothes, once the money start coming in we all going to get new wardrobes and donate our clothes to the church that are still decent."

"Bet. I can't wait to go shopping. I'll see you guys later, I'm going to get the stuff together we're going to donate." Desi said and left the room running up the stairs.

"Me too, Neek, I'm just glad we're moving I don't care about the clothes. Except for the new Air Jordan's. Can you buy them for me, Neek?"

"Sure, go ahead and start packing and I'll take you shopping as soon as I can."

When X ran upstairs as fast as Desi, Willa looked at Neek. "All of this is happening so fast. I wish we didn't have to be a part of your press conferences."

"Mama everything is going to be okay. Davie knows about our past, so since he's not worried about it neither should we."

"I hope you're right, Neek. I don't know if I like the idea of a makeover neither."

"Mama, you're still young. Stop hiding behind mistakes you can't change. This is a new start for all of us. You have a good heart, and nothing would please me more than for you to find the right man to love you."

"Neek, your dad was the love of my life. I never was able to get him to tell me why he left us. Don't get me started on Xavier. I should have known better, and I did, but at that point I stop caring about myself. I was devastated by your dad's leaving us. I blamed myself and my self-esteem took a big hit."

"Mama, it wasn't your fault. Dad left because of his inner demons not something that you did. I know he loved all of us."

Tears slowly ran down Willa's face. "Neek, I miss him so much. Sometimes it's hard for me to even get out of the bed."

"It will be alright, Mama. Once we get settled in and you don't have to work anymore you can travel or do some of the things that will make you happy."

"Neek, you really wouldn't mind if I go away for a little while. I just need to find myself again, so I can be a better mother to all of you. I want so badly to repair my relationship with Desi."

"It will happen, Mama. Desi is just acting out because she doesn't know how to deal with losing dad and grandma."

"I know. That is why I suggested we go into counseling."

"Let's sleep on this, Mama. I will talk to her. Even if she doesn't want to go it would be good for you. Now let's get some rest." Neek and Willa said good night and headed for their bedrooms.

<u>Chapter Twenty</u>

The next morning after his workout, Neek showered and dressed. He only had a half hour before he was supposed to meet with Pastor Nate. With all that was going on in his life he needed spiritual guidance. Neek had so many emotions going on right now he didn't know where to turn at times. He could talk to Nell about anything, but sometimes it was hard to be around Nell because after his breakup with his last girl it hardened him. He wasn't as nice to women as he should be. His friend was on a collision course of self-preservation. Neek hoped one day soon Nell would meet the right girl and fall in love again. In his head he needed to get off this subject because try as he might he couldn't get Monica off his mind. He hoped that God would look out for her and that Ghost wouldn't harm her. As he was walking out the door his cell phone rang with an unknown number.

"Good morning, this is Neek." Neek knew he had to answer all his calls because he didn't know when it may be something or someone ready to take his career to the next level.

"Neek, I'm so sorry."

"Who is this? I can't hear you speak up."

"I know you haven't forgotten about me already. I said I'm sorry, Neek."

Neek stopped in his tracks when he finally recognized Monica' voice. "Monica, we have nothing to discuss. Please don't call me again."

"You're not going to accept my apology, Neek?"

"I think it's best if we never talk or see each other again. Bye Monica. Have a nice life." Neek ended the call and left to keep his appointment with Pastor Nate.

"When Neek arrived at the church he sat in the car for a few minutes before he went in. The call from Monica disturbed him. In the back of his mind he expected her to reach out to him, but when it happened all he felt was anger all over again. She acted like she didn't know how badly she hurt him. Every time it seems like he was over her something happens to pull him right back in. He didn't want to get back with her, but he also didn't want to see her hurt by Ghost or anyone else. Realizing he better get into the church Neek left his car and went inside. He went straight back to Pastor Nate's office per Pastor Nate's instructions since he told Neek his secretary was out for the day. Knocking on the door, Neek was told to enter.

"Hi, Pastor Nate, hope all is well with you."

"Come on in, Domineek and have a seat."

"Thanks for seeing me on short notice. I just needed someone to bounce some things off."

"I told you, Neek, my doors are always open for you and the family."

"Speaking of the family, after dinner last night we had a long discussion about how much our lives are about to change."

"Yes, it is. You must stay strong to your faith, Domineek. You are going to be put under a lot of pressure. Money can be a blessing or can be the root to all evil. Be wise and stay humble."

"I'm trying my best. There is so much going on. I'm going to be signing with Nike very soon. I thought I would have until after Draft Day to start making big money, but with the deal with Nike, I'm going from a young man with barely five hundred dollars in his account to a multi-millionaire."

"It's going to rough having to deal with that kind of money, but Davie is a savvy businessman. He will be able to help you build your financial portfolio."

"I know. We have already started working on that. Another thing I didn't expect to happen is that he wants the family to be part of some of the press conferences. I'm a little worried that Mama and Desi will let their bad feelings towards each other out in the open for everyone to see."

"Domineek, I love all three of you guys like you were my own, but Desi needs help to deal with her pinned up anger issues."

"I know. Mama has been trying to get her to go into counseling with her, but Desi refuses."

"You have to try to convince her, Domineek. It would help if she starts with bible classes. Once she is on the right spiritual path that will help her tremendously."

"I'll keep working on her. Another thing that came up in the meeting was about our moving. This is tough because I don't know what team I'll be signing with so moving somewhere with an extended lease isn't the answer. I've been looking at condos, townhouses, and apartments in the metro Detroit area."

"Why are you worried about leasing when you can just buy a house or a condo?"

"If I do that what happens if I'm signed with another out of state team?"

"You can use it as an investment property. Michigan will always be your home. If or when you sign with another team there are times when you will have to come back so when you do you don't have to worry about where you would stay."

"You're right, Pastor Nate. I didn't think of it along those lines. That is why I wanted to build a powerful support team. What you all have brought into my life words can't express how much I appreciate all of you."

"Domineek, you need to realize you bring just as much or more into everyone life. Your family is blessed to have you looking out for them and so is Nell."

"Nell is someone else I'm concerned about. Ever since he broken up with his girl last year he seemed to have changed towards women. He has hardened. I think he is drinking too much too."

"There is only so much you can do to help him. Just continued to let him know you are in his corner."

"I was finally able to talk him into letting me get better housing for him and maybe a better car. He is like a brother to me. I just want him to know that I have his back."

"Keep up the good work, Domineek. Now I better let you go to tend to your business. Let me know how things turn out for you."

"One more thing, Pastor Nate, will you attend Draft Day with us?"

"I'll be honored."

"Just to give you a heads up you may be asked to do a few interviews, will that be a problem?"

"Not if it's not a problem with you."

"Cool, I'll let you know the details when everything has been arranged. Don't worry about expenses, Davie got that covered." Neek stood and shook Pastor Nate's hand before leaving with a clearer mind and a better outlook for his future.

Chapter Twenty-One

Later that evening Neek was resting from his busy day. He didn't know how players found time to cheat on their spouses/significant others when the schedule Davie had him on was exhausting. He was glad for that because when he was focus on his workouts he didn't have time think about Monica. He wondered if he would ever get over her. He had to catch himself because at one point he hoped Ghost dogged her out. He truly knew how his mom felt when their dad left. Monica was his first real love. The girls and women he dated before Monica couldn't compare to what she brought into his life. Neek slightly jumped when his cell phone rang.

"Hello, this is Neek."

"Neek, we have our work cut out for us. The Nike officials has schedule a Press Conference for Friday afternoon after we officially sign the contract with them on Friday morning."

Sitting up in his bed, Neek asked, "The contract signing is set up for this Friday?"

"Yes. Tomorrow is going to be a big day. We're going to arrange for your family to be prep. We will take care of everything, they just have to make themselves available for the entire day."

"But my mom is still working until the end of the week."

"She needs to quit today. We can't have the mother of the first round overall draft pick working. She is going to have to be available when we need her. By the way I will need you here at the office at eight o'clock on Thursday morning to go over financial planning." Davie said.

"I thought you didn't want me to deviate from my workout schedule."

"Neek, things in the industry change from day to day. You're going to have to be ready at a moment notice if an unexpected event happens."

"No problem, Davie. I better go talk to my family to let them know that life as we knew it is a passing fancy."

"You're right about that. By the way I put a team on looking for housing. They should have some properties for your family to view shortly."

"Wait a minute, Davie. I have already started looking for us a place."

"You will not have time to be bother with things like that. If you like your family could work with the search, but you my dear boy is going to be way too busy for such projects."

"Thanks for calling, Davie. I need to prepare my family for the latest events. I'll talk to you tomorrow."

"Get some sleep. I'm going to need you to bring your A game for all that is happening this week."

"Sure will. Goodnight, Davie." Neek ended his call with Davie and headed downstairs to talk to his family.

When Neek went downstairs Willa and X was in the den watching TV. Desi was nowhere in sight. Neek went back upstairs to see if she was in her room. When he knocked on her door she told him to come in. Desi had always kept an untidy room, but clothes were thrown everywhere, and boxes laid around on the floor.

"Desi what is all of this?" Neek asked.

"I was going through my things to see what and where to make donations."

"I need you to stop right now and come downstairs with me. I have to talk to all of you."

Desi happily stop what she was doing. She prayed Neek was going to tell them they would be moving soon and could go shopping. "What about, Neek?"

"Just come downstairs and find out." Neek left Desi's room, but he knew she wouldn't be far behind. Once they all were together, Neek filled them in on Davie's call.

"I just got a call from Davie. We are going to sign my contract with Nike on Friday morning and that afternoon we're going to have a Press Conference."

"Neek, I have to work on Friday." Willa said.

"No, Mama. You're not going back to work. Let them know that you're not coming back. Tomorrow Davie is going to set up, so we can prep for the Press Conference."

"I can't go on TV with my hair looking like this." Desi said.

"You won't have to. Davie is going to take care of your hair, makeup, and wardrobe."

"Oh my God. So that means we are going to be on TV." Willa asked.

"Yes, Mama. I'm going to need you and Desi to be on your best behavior. I can't stress enough how important it is."

"I don't know if I want to be on TV, Neek." X said.

"It will be alright, man. We all going to be there to support you. Another thing, Mama. You may have to work with some people to find us housing. I told Davie I could do that, but he said I won't have time."

"So, we're going to be moving soon." Desi asked in excitement.

"Yes, we are. Now if you guys don't have any more questions then I want to go and find Nell."

"Neek, can I go with you?" X asked.

"Sorry, man. It's too late for you to be out. I'll see you in the morning. I think all of you guys should get some rest tonight because from the way it sounds, we're going to be very busy over the next few days."

"You don't have to tell me twice. I want to look well rested for my close-up." Desi said.

"But Neek said the Press Conference isn't until Friday, Desi." X said.

"It doesn't matter. A girl can never get too much rest; besides I have to get to all the old stuff I won't be needing any longer."

"You are so extra girl." Neek said.

"I love you too, big brother." Desi ran upstairs much quicker than she came down.

"You're going to create a monster if you give that girl everything she wants." Willa said.

"Mama all of us deserve to live better. We have done without for a long time so it's nothing wrong with splurging a little."

"Yeah, Mama. We're not going to become brats." X said then thought for a few seconds. "At least I'm not going to."

Giving his mom a hug and his little brother dap, Neek left the house in search of Nell.

Chapter Twenty-Two

Neek sat in the car in front of his house. He was waiting on Nell to call him back. He was really worried about Nell. They were not able to hang out as much since Neek started his new schedule. He hoped Nell didn't feel like he didn't want to spend time with him. He explained to Nell when he got his schedule that he was going to be busy for a while. Neek was worried that Nell was partying and drinking too much. He also was worried about where he was getting money from because Nell wasn't working, and his family didn't have money to spare. Coming out of his thoughts when his phone rang he was happy to see that it was Nell.

"Hey, man what's up. I've been trying to holla at you."

Nell was quite for a little while. Neek thought their call was disconnected. "I've been here and there." Nell said.

"You can come at me better than that, man."

"What do you want, Neek."

"I want to meet up with you to go over a few things."

"I don't know when I'm free. I'll get back at you after I check."

"We missed you at the last meeting. A lot been going on. I need to give you some updates."

"I'll holla at you tomorrow, Neek."

"What are you doing now, Nell, this is kind of important."

"Why is it important, Neek, because you said so?"

"Nell what's going on with you, man?"

"I told you I'll holla at you tomorrow." Nell ended their call before Neek could say anything else.

Sitting in his car wondering what the hell was wrong with his best friend, Neek decided to call Coach Rodgers. "Hey Coach, you have a few minutes to chat?"

"Sure, Neek, what's on your mind?"

"I just had the strangest conversation with Nell."

"What was strange about it?"

"It seemed like he was angry with me."

Coach Rodgers was quiet then said, "Why do you think he was angry with you?"

"It was his tone of voice and the fact that he didn't want to meet up with me."

"When was the last time you saw Nell?"

Neek had to think for a few minutes. "I can't really say. My days seem to run together, but I think I only saw him once briefly since we went out to celebrate with Davie."

"Neek, you can't make Nell's problems yours."

"What do you mean by Nell's problems?"

"I think something is eating away at him, Neek. I noticed it at the luncheon."

"Why didn't you say something, Coach? Nell is family. I want to help him out any way I can."

"That's just it, Neek. Have you ever thought about how Nell feels with everything that's going on in your life?"

"I don't understand, if Nell has a problem with me he would have said something."

"Let me ask you a question, Neek. If the shoes were on Nell's feet instead of yours would you feel left out?"

"So now you're saying I'm leaving Nell out, Coach." Neek was getting a little upset with this conversation.

"Not intentionally, but you are a very busy man and things are only going to get worse as Draft Day heads closer. I'm sure that you have offered to help Nell out financially."

"He wouldn't let me do anything for him but get him housing and maybe a better car. But none of that should matter. Nell is my brother in every way that counts I want to help him."

"What about what Nell wants, Neek?"

"He is not being open with me, so I don't know what he wants any longer. I hope he doesn't let this drive him down a crazy path of no return."

"Neek, this is going to be hard, but I need you to listen to me. You can't save everyone."

"Coach, I'm not trying to save everyone. I just want to take care of my family and friends."

"That's what you want, Neek, but you have to think. Not everyone will see your jesters are ok. Personally, I would feel that way if you tried to lavish money or gifts upon me."

"So, you're saying you're not going to take any money or gifts from me?"

"Not personal gifts. If you want to make donations to the school I'm cool with that."

"But what about all the time you have dedicated to me with finding an agent and assisting with the contracts?"

"I see that as part of my coaching responsibilities. Do you know how much press we're going to get from you? Our school is going to be known nationally for having the number one overall NBA Draft pick."

"This suck. I wanted to help you and Pastor Nate for all you have done for me. I didn't get where I am by myself."

"No great star does. If I were you I will check with Pastor Nate if you planned monetary or other gifts for him. Your donation to the church well compensates the time he spends supporting you."

"You gave me a lot to think about, Coach. I better head back in the house since I'm not going to meet up with Nell tonight. Thanks for giving me something to think about."

"You're welcome. Have a good night, Neek."

"You too, Coach." Neek ending his call and went back into the house.

Chapter Twenty-Three

The next day Neek was up bright and early. Davie called to let him know to have the family at the DAG offices, so they could start with the prep for the Press Conference. He said after that he had a realtor friend to take Willa and the rest of the family around to find housing. Neek would be meeting with Davie's financially team that afternoon instead of the next day. He was determined that Neek knew from the beginning how to invest his money wisely. Davie knew all of this had to be overwhelming for Neek. Here is a kid from the roughest streets of Detroit without two nickels to scratch together about to become a multi-millionaire in a few days.

Neek remember the conversation he had with Davie that morning. He was extra upset that Neek didn't tell him that Monica had tried to contact him days ago. He told Neek he had to know everything that happens in his life good or bad, so he could get in front of it if there was a need. Their conversation didn't start off on a pleasant note.

"Hey, Davie. We will be heading over that way soon."

"Never mind that. Why in the hell you didn't tell me that you have been communicating with your ex." Davie yelled.

"Hold up one damn minute, Davie. You don't get to talk to me in that tone."

"I warned you that she was going to be sniffing around, I need to know these things, so I can take care of it right away."

"I talked to Monica one time since signing with you, Davie. She called me, I told her to get lost so that is the end of the story."

"It doesn't work that way, Neek. Do you think she going to just let you go now that you are about to cash in on millions?"

"That girl in the last person on my mind. My focus is to take care of my family and to be the best ball player I can be, so my dad's hard work won't be in vain."

"That's good to hear, Neek. What else have you been holding back from me?"

"I haven't been holding back anything. Listen, Davie we need to get a few things straight. I will follow your lead when it comes to business, but when it comes to my personal life you need to back off."

"Don't play with me, Neek. I've shown you stacks of documents where young players have so much potential, but it is blown to hell because there were no safeguards put into play to shut down personal issues from the past."

"I'm an open book, Davie."

"Okay, what's going on with your best friend?"

"Nell is good. Why are you asking about him?"

"It seems he has a problem with drinking. Funny I didn't pick that up at the luncheon."

"What are you talking about, Davie?"

"Well it seems that your friend has been involve in a few bar fights."

"That can't be true. Nell is a light drinker and he doesn't go to bars."

"That's not what his DPD report says."

"I have to go, Davie. See you shortly." Neek ended their call.

Now that the family was sitting in a small conference room at DAG, Neek excused himself to call Nell. He wanted Nell to be a part of this, so he hoped he was able to talk Nell into meeting them there. Nell finally answered the phone on the fourth ring.

"Nell are you still in bed. It's almost ten o'clock. What happened to the earlier riser?" Neek asked.

"You woke me up to ask me some silly questions like that, man.?"

"No, I wanted to see if you would join us at DAG. They are prepping us for the Press Conference that's going to take place this Friday after I sign with Nike."

"Good luck, Neek. I proud of you man."

"You're my brother, Nell. I want you to be with us every step of the way."

"No can do, Neek."

"What's going on, Nell?"

"I've decided I needed to take a step back, so you can shine."

"You're not making sense, Nell."

"Neek, you don't know how hard it is to be me. I'm getting all this attention from the honeys just because I'm your best friend."

"Nell that's not true. You are great in your field. You don't have to live in my shadow."

"I know that's why I think we need to chill. I just want to have fun this summer and finish my last year of school, so I can get the hell out of Michigan."

"Nell, stop talking crazy, man. We have had each other's back since we were kids."

"Now we're grown ass men that need to be aware of what is going on around us. I don't want to be known as Neek's poor black friend."

"Nell, I have to go right now. I'll holla at you later. Can you drop by the crib tonight?"

"Sure bye, Neek."

"Holla at you later, man." Neek went back to the rest of the family. He was now worried about Nell even more. He wasn't making sense and still in bed this late in the day. Maybe Davie was right he needed to find out what was going on with Nell.

Chapter Twenty-Four

The long and exhausting day was finally over. Neek was so proud of how well his family handled themselves at the prepping. He was elated that his mom was so happy. He hadn't seen her smile so much since his dad left them. He hoped this experience would bring her out of her shell. He also couldn't believe after looking at several properties she finally settled on a four bedroom, with four baths condo in Novi. The way her eyes brighten up when she talked about the new place made Neek want to cry. Desi and X was elated because their bedroom would have their own private bath. For the first time in years it seemed at thought his mom and sister was trying to get along.

Neek told them to have an early night since they would have to be up around six to finish up their final prepping and go shopping for the Press Conference. Neek sat downstairs in the kitchen waiting on Nell to show up. He was already an hour late. Neek told him if he couldn't make it there within the next hour they could get together the next day. Nell promised Neek he would be there in twenty minutes. Hearing the slight knock at his door Neek went to let Nell in before he woke up the rest of the family. When they sat down at the kitchen table, Neek realized that Davie may have been right about Nell getting into fights since he was sporting a black eye.

"What the hell happen to you, Nell?"

"I walked into a door." Nell said then started laughing.

"This isn't funny, Nell. Why are you doing this to yourself?"

"What am I doing, Neek but having fun? I'm still young. I want to enjoy my life.'

"You don't have to drink yourself into a stupor to have fun, Nell."

"What do you know about having fun, Neek? You are so focused on doing the right thing all the time your life is going to just pass you by."

"Why are you so angry with me, Nell, we're brothers?"

"Neek, I can't deal with living in your shadow. Do you know how many people that wouldn't give me the time of day wants to be all up in my grill now, so they can get next to you?"

"Man, I didn't know all of this was going on. Why didn't you tell me?"

Nell put his head down and thought for a few minutes. "Neek, I'm sorry I went off the deep end. I just didn't know how to handle all the people that were up in my face since the news leaked out you was going pro."

To Neek surprise Nell started sobbing. "You should have come and talked to me, man. I didn't realize any of this was going on."

"I know. I just let all of this get into my head. I appreciate all that you have done for me."

"Nell, I need to ask you something and I need for you to be totally honest with me."

"Okay, shoot."

"Does it bother you when I offer you money or gifts?"

"Most of the time it doesn't, but sometimes I feel like a leach."

"I wish you didn't feel that way. How about we make a deal? Outside of the apartment and car we talked about, I won't approach you about buying you anything or giving you money unless you ask."

"Okay, that sounds reasonable. I just don't want to feel indebted."

"Understood, if you like we could draw up an agreement and you can pay me back whenever you can afford to. But don't get it twisted; I don't want anything I give to you to be treated as a loan. I just want my brother back."

"Okay, man, stop all the whining." Nell said with a smile on his face.

"You can start looking anytime for a new place. By the time Friday gets here we are going to be rich. Mama has already gotten us a condo in Novi."

"So, Friday is the big day?"

"Yes. We prepped most of the day and will continue tomorrow. You are welcome to join us. I told the powers that be that you are to be included in any family function that is given."

"Thanks, Neek. I think I will sit this one out." Nell said as he pointed to his eye. "This will heal before you know it. I would like to attend Draft Day. Who knows, maybe I can pick up some more honeys."

"If you change your mind makeup can work wonders. I'm glad we cleared the air, Nell. I don't want to overstep. I just want to be able to take care of the people I care about. I know if the shoe was on the other foot you would look out for me too."

"You're right, man. Goodnight. I'll holla at you tomorrow."

"Goodnight, Nell." Neek walked Nell to his car and headed to bed feeling like the weight of the world had been lifted off his shoulders.

<u>Chapter Twenty-Five</u>

Tomorrow was the big day that Neek will sign the contract with Nike. In less than a week it will be Draft Day. Davie told Neek that his family will be prepped for Draft Day too, but it would go a little more smoothly since they already had the prepping for the signing. Neek was due to meet Davie and Coach Rodgers in an hour. They will be going over once again the contract from Nike. Neek couldn't believe Davie was even able to talk the shoe company into letting Neek have his own signature shoe. That wasn't part of the original deal, but since Neek's social media presence and the high-volume press surrounding Draft Day, Nike realized they had to sweeten their offer.

Now sitting in the conference room with Davie, Coach Rodgers, and the financial advisor Neek worked with yesterday, Skylar Dubois they were hard at work reviewing the numbers before tomorrow's signing. These numbers were mind blowing to Neek. Trying to understand the materials Skylar went over yesterday was a bit much. She told him to relax because after the deal is sign the financial portfolio she will put together for him will be easier to read and understand.

"So, Sky if I remember correctly from our meeting yesterday you said that in my financial portfolio my incomes will be recorded separately?"

"Yes, the BRI (Basketball Related Income), endorsements, interviews etc. will be recorded within a breakdown analysis. We're bless that you are signing the deal with Nike before Draft Day, because that mean teams will have to automatically offer extensions to your rookie contract. Is that correct, Davie."

"Pretty much. That is why we must be open minded about who you signed with, Neek."

"I understand, but I still want to be a Piston if you can make that happen." Neek said.

"I'm glad you all are working with, Neek. He is a bright young man with a great future. I don't want to see or hear about him ten years from now pushing carts at Walmart's." Coach Rodgers said.

"I take care of my athletes, Coach Rodgers. I know that is why you brought Neek here in the first place."

"Let's talk about this deal with Nike. I want to make sure that we all are on the same page. The offer states that they want to sign me to a seven-year eighty million contract with a signing bonus of four million and a guaranteed first year of twelve million. Not to mention my own shoe label." Neek clarified.

"That's correct, Neek. You also may have a possible lifetime option with them if we agreed to an extension." Davie said.

"So, you're saying tomorrow Neek will be getting the first year payment from Nike after the signing." Coach Rodgers asked.

"Yes, he will also be paid for doing the Press Conference, but that will have nothing to do with the contract. Next week after the Draft we will have a better grasp on his BRI."

"We have already schedule a meeting for the following Monday after the Draft." Sky said.

"Neek it seems like you are in great hands. I know with your keen head for numbers you will do just fine diversifying your financial portfolio." Coach Rodgers said.

"Okay, if that is all I would like to catch up with my family to see how they are holding up with the Press Conference prep and makeovers."

"Yes, we can wrap this up for now. Neek, I will see you later" Davie said. He picked up his papers and left the conference room with Skylar following behind him.

"Oh my God, Coach. I don't know how to go from rags to riches overnight. All of this seems unreal." Neek said.

"It's real, Neek. Just make sure you don't burn yourself out. You may have a handle on things right now, but once the season starts your life will never be the same and you're not going to have much free time on your hands."

"I know. That is why I want to do as much as I can with the family now. I want this badly, but I still feel that I'm letting the family down."

"Cut that out right now, man. You are doing a great job of taking care of your family. You are so used to putting their needs before yours that you are losing tract of what counts the most: TAKING CARE OF YOURSELF."

"I'll feel so much better once the family have settled in. I sure hope this move will work out better for Desi. She is doing better since she stopped hanging out with her 'friends,' but it's going to be a big adjustment for all of us to live in an upper-class neighborhood."

"They will be just find, Neek and so will you. I'm glad you were able to work things out with Nell. I know you guys go back a long way."

"Coach, how could I not see that Nell was struggling? He has no reason to feel like he is living in my shadow."

"Yes, he does, Neek. You are going to open the doors for a lot of people. Nobody that is close to you will have the same life as they use to. You need to accept right now that good and bad will come from your RISE TO FAME."

"I just want to be a normal person and play the game I love, take care of my family and friends, and finish my degree. I don't need all of this attention."

"It's too late. You're going to get so much more after tomorrow. I suggest you be ready for people to come out of the woodwork to get a piece of you."

"Coach before you leave I need to say one more thing to you. Like I told Nell last night, I want to share my wealth with the people I care about. I didn't realize how others would feel when I want to do something special for them." Neek paused for a few seconds and continued. "I would like to help you out personally and had every intention of doing so until we had that talk about you're not wanting anything like that from me. If you ever need anything, please just say the word. I won't force gifts or money on you."

"I appreciate that, man. I'm just happy things are finally going your way."

"Will you at least let me buy you gifts for your birthday and Christmas? I promise not to go overboard."

"Now that will work. We better get out of here. I have to head back over to the gym."

"Thanks, Coach. I will see you at the prepping for the Press Conference." Neek and Coach Rodgers left the conference room. Neek going to prep with his family and Coach Rodgers back to the gym.

Chapter Twenty-Six

When Neek woke up the next morning he was anxious. The idea of becoming a millionaire by the end of the day was out of this world. He was going to budget wise especially when it came to Desi. She was at the age where she thinks the sky is the limit. Neek had to agree with his mom that Desi wasn't as mature as she claimed. They will be signing the paperwork on their new condo tomorrow morning. He told the family the items they were taking with them would be moved by professional movers. Sometime over the weekend Willa, Desi, and X was going to go shopping for the condo. Again, Davie hired a team to help them out with that project. Neek didn't care how or what they brought as long as he had a comfortable bed to sleep in.

The rest of the family had been picked up already, so they could work with the people that would get them ready. It was important to Neek to get his workout in that morning more so then any other morning because after his workout he felt energized for the rest of the day. Neek hoped Nell would change his mind and show up for the signing, because he wanted all his family there. At least he felt grateful that Coach Rodgers and Pastor Nate would be there. They didn't like the fact that they had to work with the team also on their appearance.

The time had come so Neek left the house that he lived in most of his life knowing that in a few days he would never return to it. Since his mom owned the house they were going to donate it to the church. They knew Pastor Nate would know what to do with it. That was one thing they were able to get after losing his dad, the house was paid off. Pulling up at the DAG offices, Neek headed to the back entrance so he wouldn't be accosted by the press. He knew they had heard about the signing taken place today. Some of the reporters that were there weren't invited to the Press Conference. Neek was ushered into a fitting room where he had to get dressed and head to Davie's office to seal the deal. The Press Conference was scheduled to be held in the large conference room.

After he was dressed and reached Davie's office, Neek was pleasantly surprised at how nice everyone looked. He knew his mom was a very pretty woman, but life had taken a toll on how she carried herself. The woman he looked at was simply beautiful. Her hair was put up on top of her head with soft silky curls flowing down the side of her face. Her makeup was flawless. The black and gray two-piece pant set she wore fitted her slender model like frame to a tee. Looking at his sister and brother almost brought tears to Neek's eyes. Desi looked like a runway model. Her shoulder length hair was wrapped around her beautifully made up face with soft flowing curls. She looked amazing in her fuchsia color dress that reached mid-thigh. The four-inch matching shoes made her above average height even taller. Finally, there was X. His baby brother rocked the hell out of his black tux. His hair was cut short and lined perfectly. After giving all of them a hug, Davie motioned for him to come to his desk where he sat with two executives from Nike.

The introductions were made. Neek sat a little nervous between Coach Rodgers and Pastor Nate, while the two executives sat on the other side of Davie.

"Neek is there anything you would like to ask or say before we get started." Davie asked.

Clearing his throat Neek said, "I would like to thank you guys on behalf of me, my family, and my support team for giving me the opportunity to sport a brand that is so important to me and my dad."

One of the executives, Oliver Sampson replied, "The pleasure is ours Domineek. We look forward to having a long and lasting relationship with you."

The other executive, Bryson Gordon, said, "This is only the beginning Domineek. We hope to expand on our business relationship for many years to come. With that being said, let's get down to business."

"Domineek Kane Williamson on behalf of Nike, I would like to present to you the contract that will bring us together for at least the next seven years." Oliver Sampson said as he handed the contract to Neek.

Neek took the contract. He looked it over to make sure all the terms were as the one he reviewed. After studying the contract, he handed it to Coach Rodgers. Coach Rodgers briefly glanced at the contract and gave it back to Neek. Before Neek signed the contract, he called Willa over to the desk. He stood and gave her a big hug. Once he sat back down he pulled a pen out of his pocket then initial and signed in the designated places. When he was finished he handed the contract back to Oliver.

It was Davie turn to take over. He handed Neek a dummy check for ten point-two million dollars. The actual money had already been deposited into an account that Neek had previously opened. Taking the check and giving it to his mom was very emotional.

"Okay, now that the business side is over with for now, it's time to eat. A buffet has been set up in the executive dining room." Myra came in right at that moment to take them to the dining room, but Davie asked Neek to stay behind. Once the others had left he asked Neek to have a seat.

"We have a problem." Davie said.

"What kind of problem, Davie?"

"Your ex showed up here earlier trying to get into the building."

"I don't know why she would do that. I haven't had any contact with her. I told her the last time we talk to not call me anymore."

"I figured something like this would happen that's why I took extra precautions."

"I'm sorry, Davie. I thought the situation was handled."

"That is why I'm going to give you one chance to handle it. I had her taken to a private room in the back. You need to shut her down for good, Neek."

"Davie, I don't have time to deal with her drama. I just want to go eat and enjoy my family and friends. With the tight schedule you have me on I'm not going to see much of them for a while."

"Neek this isn't optional. See what she wants and end this once and for all. She will be escorted off the property once you're done."
"Thanks for the heads up, Davie."

"I will have your back, Neek. Myra will take you to where Monica is waiting."

Neek was taken to the room where Monica was sitting on a nice plush chair. She didn't look like the well dress woman he'd seen since she hooked up with Ghost, instead she was plainly dress with no makeup. Neek was finally content with himself because he didn't feel nothing for the person that sat in front of him.

"What the hell are you doing here, Monica?"

"I need to talk to you, Neek."

"I have nothing to say to you but stay the hell out of my life."

"I made a mistake, Neek. I'm sorry. I know we can work things out."

"Girl, you lost your mind if you think that you can crawl back to me after you been with that fool."

"Please, Neek. I just want the chance to make all of this up to you."

"Monica, this is the last time I'm going to tell you to step. Security will escort you to your car." Neek said and turn to leave.

"I don't' have a car, Neek. I don't have anything. Ghost left me, and my family won't let me come back home."

"Not my problem. Goodbye, Monica." Neek left the room without turning back to look at the defeated look on Monica's face.

Chapter Twenty-Seven

By the time Neek made it to the Press Conference the room was nearly full. Entering through the back entrance, Neek headed for the table and was happy beyond words when he saw Nell was seated in the row behind the table sitting next to his family, Coach Rodgers, and Pastor Nate. The makeup artist worked wonders because you couldn't even tell Nell had a black eye. Nell looked good in his grey suit. When Neek sat down next to Davie he slightly smiled when Davie whispered, "How is that project coming along?"

"It's a go, Davie." That was all Neek had time to say before Oliver stood to address the press.

"Ladies and gentlemen, it is with pleasure I announce that there have been an agreement reached between Nike and the soon to be overall first round draft pick, Domineek Kane Williamson." Oliver had Neek to stand up and presented him with an oversized blank check.

With the cameras flashing and the reporters trying to get their questions in at one time was out of control for a while until Bryson was able to calm the crown somewhat, so questions could be heard. The first question was directed at Davie.

"Mr. Greene, how sure are you that Neek will be the number one overall draft pick?"

"We are very confident. There is no other college player out there today that can come close to Neek's ball handling skills, scoring, and most of all extensive knowledge of the game."

The second question was also directed at Davie. "What team do you think will draft Neek?"

"There are several possibilities. We're going to keep our options open and wait for the offer that will be best for Neek's career not just his rookie years."

Another reporter yelled. "What are the terms of Neek's contact with Nike?"

"That isn't something we can divulge at this time." Bryson said. After about ten more questions were asked and answered by Davie, Oliver, and Bryson, Davie took over and told the press only one more question would be answered.

"You stated in your media bliss of how Neek is an upstanding man on and off the court. What kind of man would leave his pregnant girlfriend in her time of need?"

The room was quiet for a while. Neek and his family looked on with shocked faces. "I'll answer that question, Davie." Neek went to stand at the center of the table, between Davie and Oliver. "I don't have a girlfriend and haven't for months now."

"That's not what Monica Jackson said. She said you walked out on her once you decided to turn pro knowing that she was carrying your baby."

"I have nothing else to say regarding this matter." Neek went back to his seat while Davie took over shutting down the conference.

Once Davie cleared the room and send the family out to shop for the condo, the others went to the conference room to address what just happened at the Press Conference. Nell, Coach Rodgers, and Pastor Nate joined the meeting with Neek, Davie, and the Nike executives.

"I thought you said you had this handled, Neek". Davie said obviously upset.

"She is pulling strings out of the air. I told her point blank we were over and to have a good life."

"And that is exactly what she is planning on doing on your dime, Neek." Davie yelled.

"Why are you blowing this out of proportion, Davie?" Oliver asked.

"It's a big deal right before the draft for Neek to be painted as a deadbeat." Davie answered.

"This is the oldest trick in book, Davie. That girl is off her rocker. She isn't a bit more pregnant that I am." Neek said.

"Well that is her word against yours. She has nothing to lose unlike you."

"Davie, Monica can't have children. She had a hysterectomy last year." Neek said.

"That's insane. If that is true, then why would she tell such an outlandish lie?"

"You just said the magic words, Davie. She is insane."

"Our work is done for now. Neek we will see you on Draft Day." Oliver and Bryson left the others in the conference room.

"That chick needs to be committed." Nell said.

"This is a cry for help." Pastor Nate said.

"I don't care what it is. We are too close to our big day for that twit to take us off our course of action." Davie said.

"Davie, we need to move on and stop giving her so much power. I need to find my family to make sure they are okay." Neek said.

"Neek this isn't going to just go away. She has to be handled." Davie said.

"So, handle it, Davie. Isn't that your specialty? Pastor Nate, could you come with me in case Mama needs to talk to you?"

"Sure, son, this isn't a good time for her." Pastor Nate said.

When Pastor Nate made that comment a sad look crossed Neek's face. He had forgotten that tomorrow would have been his dad's forty-first birthday. "I have to go, Davie. Nell, Coach Rodgers, I'll holla at you guys later." Neek and Pastor Nate left the office in search of his family.

Chapter Twenty-Eight

It was finally Draft Day. Neek and his family was so glad to be there. They had a few hurdles to climb after Monica pulled her stunt at the Press Conference. Neek didn't like the way Davie handled the situation but at least it was handled. He made sure the public knew about Monica's hysterectomy. He also made sure the reported that asked the question was fired for not validating his information. Everything else was going as planned. The family moved into their condo. Pastor Nate was in the process of getting the house ready for a family that was recently burnt out of their home and lost everything to move in.

Nell was back to his old self. He had pre-registered for his fall classes at U of M, moved into his new apartment only a few miles from the university, and started an internship at one of the biggest electronics companies in Michigan. Neek still worked out with Coach Rodgers when he had the free time. Neek was still close to his support group. The Nike shoe deal also kept Neek busy. His biggest problem with the deal was that he had to wear hats. So, when he had to be in full Nike attire he wasn't a happy camper.

That morning Neek went out to breakfast with his family, support team, and Davie. They couldn't eat much because they all were too excited to eat. Neek made a toast. "Family and friends the day has finally come where we're going to find out where our next chapter is going to start."

"Neek, man, I know you're not about to get all sappy on us." Nell said.

"Let my son talk, Nell." Willa said with a smile on her face.

"Anyway, as I was saying. I wouldn't have made it this far without everyone in this room."

"What did I do, Neek?" X asked.

"You've been a big help looking out for Mama and Desi when I was so busy." Neek answered.

"Don't get it twisted, Neek. I don't need anyone looking out for me." Desi said.

"Yes, you do, baby girl, it's been a big adjustment for all of us, I must say I' proud of you Desi for not letting surplus money go to your head." Neek said.

"Oh yes she did. Look how big her head is now." X said and everyone at the table laughed hysterically.

"That's enough, X. Leave your sister alone." Willa said. She and Desi's relationship had gotten a whole lot better.

"I'll like to make a toast next. It has really been a pleasure getting to know your family better, Neek. Getting to know someone on your own is so much more rewarding than listening to rumors or research. I've learned so much since you signed on with my firm. My toast is to new beginnings." Davie said.

"Pastor Nate, it's time to get going. Can you lead us with a closing prayer?" Neek asked.

"Sure. Thank you, Lord, for your presence with us on this day. As we depart to see this young man take his place in life, we ask you to bless us throughout the remainder of the day and guide us safely to our destination. Do not let what we have learnt here today die, but instead, may we continue to ruminate within us throughout the year, until we find ourselves together again. WE ask this in the name of Jesus, and in the power of the Holy Spirit. Amen."

"Thank you, Pastor Nate. We better head to the center." Neek said as they left the restaurant with peace in their hearts.

The group made it to the center about half hour before the number one overall pick was to be announced. All the hype boiled down to this special moment. Neek sat between his mom and sister. Suddenly for the first time since he made the decision to leave school early, Neek was concerned about not being the number one overall pick. He knew it was just nerves so he let all that fly right out of his mind. Now that the time had come, Neek held his breath and listened to the announcer.

"With the first pick in the 2018 NBA Draft the Atlanta Hawks pick from University of Detroit Mercy, Domineek Kane Williamson."

Neek sat there for a few seconds until his mom and sister jumped up yelling excitingly. Neek stood and went to the podium with Davie following behind him. Everything after that went by in a flash. Neek didn't know what he said. He did remember his family coming up there to join him. The next thing he knew he was confronted by the press asking tons of questions.

"Neek what are your thoughts about being selected by the Atlanta Hawks when your dream was to be a Detroit Piston?"

My dream is to play basketball. Yes, it was important to me and my dad for me to be a Detroit Piston, but some things are out of your control. In the end no matter where I play I will do so with the drive and determination I learnt from my dad, basketball camps, and high school and college coaches."

"What made you decide to turn pro after years of pursuit by NBA teams earlier in your college years?"

"I felt in my heart the time was right. I have every intention of finishing my education, but for right now this decision was best for me and my family."

"Okay, that's enough for now. You will have more opportunities soon to get your questions answered." Davie ushered Neek and the other out before any additional questions could be asked.

Epilogue

One year later

It was off season. Neek had to fly out to keep his commitments to the team. He enjoyed his first year with the Atlanta Hawks even though they were knocked out of the playoffs in the first round. Individually Neek enjoyed being Rookie of the Year and making it to the All-Star Game. His stats were even higher than his college stats. He dated infrequently because he didn't want to get caught up in any drama like he had with Monica. He decided a long time ago to remember her the way she was the first few years of their relationship. He felt bad for her family that she had lost her way so completely she took her own life. Ghost demised came when he got into a turf war with another drug lord. Again, Neek tried to remember the kid he was friends with so many years ago.

Finding out how bad Ghost had treated Monica angered Neek, but he had to let all that go. Nell graduated with honors from U of M a few months ago. Neek couldn't talk him into moving to Atlanta, but he was happy that Nell finally had a special woman to share his life with. What was so amazing about Nell's relationship with Camille was that he'd known her since his freshman year at U of M, but they were just friends. When Nell went back to school last fall they started seeing each other and now they were inseparable.

Desi was now a senior in high school. She had thrived well since they moved to Atlanta. She didn't show any signs of reverted back to her old ways and no one would ever be able to tell that she and their mom had a rocky relationship a while ago. X would be attending middle school in the fall. He kept active by playing soccer and his latest interest karate. He was great at it mastering his belts in record time.

Coach Rodgers finally settled down and got married to a woman he had been dating off and on for three years. They were expecting their first baby in seven months. Pastor Nate was still heavily involved in the church. Neek was able to meet the nice family that Pastor Nate gave their old house to. He was so happy for them and they were so grateful for the gift.

The biggest and most difficult change over the last year came from Willa. Neek was glad when she started showing interest in men again, but when he found out that she was involved with Davie he flipped out. He had gotten a funny feeling when Davie made the toast right before Draft Day, but he put it down to his nerves. He told Davie it wasn't good for their business relationship for him to be dating his mom, but his mom and Davie told Neek their relationship didn't have anything to do with their business relationship.

Now that Neek had finished his first year in the NBA and had more money then he'll ever be able to spend, he thought about what he was going to do when he finished in the NBA. He didn't know if he would feel like he felt now that he'll want to leave the NBA behind when his four-year contract was up with the Hawks. All he knew was that he was itching to finish his degree and live his second dream of becoming an engineer. When someone suggested he should get a book written about his life a title popped into his head. Neek went into his study and after booting up his laptop he typed in big bold letters: **THE MAKING OF A LEGEND: NEEK'S RISE TO FAME.**

Discussion Questions

Listed below are discussion questions your book club may be interested in discussing:

1) Why do you think Neek struggled so hard with whether to go pro?

2) Do you think Neek's decision would have been easier if he wasn't worried about his family, Monica, and Nell?

3) What do you think about the roles Nell, Coach Rodgers, and Pastor Nate played in Neek's life?

4) Do you think Desi was justified for being angry with Willa?

5) What do you think about Neek, Nell, and Ghost's relationship?

6) Do you think is was realistic for Neek to base his life's decisions on what he thought he dad wanted?

7) Why do you think Monica couldn't wait on Neek to finish his degree and not pressure him to turn pro?

8) Do you think Nell's feelings of living in Neek's shadow was accurate?

9) When Monica went to Neek before the Press Conference apologizing for her treatment of him, do you feel he was too hard on her?

10) Do you feel that Willa and Davie were right that their personal relationship had nothing to do with Davie's business relationship with Neek?

11) If there should be a sequel to this book, which character would be the best character to continue the series?

12) What do you think should be Neek's next move for his career? Do you think he should settle down and start a family?

Dear Reader,

I hope you enjoyed reading *The Making of a Legend: Neek's Rise to Fame.* This book was written as a suggestion by a dear friend, Annie McGee. Diana likes to keep her readers entertained by writing something that is satisfying and inspirational. Thank you for taking the time out to read this book.

It would be greatly appreciated if you would consider writing a review of this title on Amazon, Barnes & Noble, and/or my website dianacarterwriter.com in the Comments section under Contact Us (located under the More tab). When you visit my website, you will be informed about upcoming events, publishing services offered, and more.

God's blessings,

Diana Carter

You can find me on the web:

Website: www.dianacarterwriter.com
Amazon Author Page: www.amazon.com/author/diana.carter
Goodreads: www.Goodreads.com/dianacarter

Author's Information

Diana Carter started her writing career after taking a personality test many years ago and disagreeing with the results. After talking to the administrator of that test, Diana was encouraged to submit the book she had written for publication. Born was her first book ***Broken Promises: Shattered Dreams*** which was published on April 10, 2014 by Outskirts Press. Look for the first three titles in the ***Broken Promises*** series and the first title in the ***Dark Revenge*** to be rewritten and published later this year.

Diana has a passion for writing fiction stories that will not only entertain her readers but also have a lasting impact. She loves to write and looks forward to continuing for many years to come. When she takes a break from writing, she likes to spend time with her children, grandchildren, bowl, read, and tutoring disadvantaged adults.

You can find additional information on Diana's website at www.dianacarterwriter.com, or by checking out her Amazon page at: amazon.com/author/diana.carter or if you like to personally reach her do so via email at diana.carter44@gmail.com.

www.ingramcontent.com/pod-product-compliance
Lightning Source LLC
Chambersburg PA
CBHW050150110726
47898CB00008B/2744